W9-AVR-142

With a groan that was part protest, part relief, Rafe gave in to the desire to taste her.

Lily's mouth was soft and pliant, and unexpectedly hot. Still finding it difficult to breathe, he pulled her even closer, plundering her willing sweetness with his tongue until he was forced to take a breath.

Her submission had been as incredible as it was eager, and when he dragged his mouth from hers, he buried his face in the hollow between her shoulder and her neck.

"Cristo," he muttered hoarsely, aware that he was near to losing it. But when she gave a little moan and wound her arms around his neck, Rafe knew he had fallen into a trap of his own making.

Dios. As he inhaled her scent, he knew he'd never dreamed that he might be seduced by her youth and inexperience. How could he have known that her lips might excite and inflame him until his body was bathed in her heat? When he'd thrust his tongue into her mouth, he'd reveled in its possession. *Querido Dios*, his control had almost been swept away.

Aware that the fire he had created was threatening to consume him, Rafe's hands curled about her nape. Her silky hair tumbled about his fingers, and he badly wanted to go on kissing her. But this was madness, he told himself. It couldn't be allowed to win.

Anne Mather and her husband live in the north of England in a village bordering the county of Yorkshire. It's a beautiful area, and she can't imagine living anywhere else. She's been making up stories since she was in primary school and would say that writing is a huge part of her life. When people ask if writing is a lonely occupation, she usually says that she's so busy sorting out her characters' lives, she doesn't have time to feel lonely. Anne's written over 160 novels, and her books have appeared on both the *New York Times* and *USA TODAY* bestseller lists. She loves reading and walking and browsing in bookshops. And now that her son and daughter are grown, she takes great delight in her grandchildren. You can email her at mystic-am@msn.com.

Books by Anne Mather

Harlequin Presents

Morelli's Mistress
Innocent Virgin, Wild Surrender
A Forbidden Temptation
His Forbidden Passion
The Brazilian Millionaire's Love-Child

Latin Lovers

Mendez's Mistress

The Greek Tycoons

The Greek Tycoon's Pregnant Wife

Wedlocked!

Jack Riordan's Baby

Passion

The Forbidden Mistress
Savage Awakening

Visit Harlequin.com for more titles.

Anne Mather

—

A DANGEROUS TASTE
OF PASSION

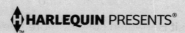
HARLEQUIN PRESENTS®

If you purchased this book without a cover you should be aware that this book is stolen property. It was reported as "unsold and destroyed" to the publisher, and neither the author nor the publisher has received any payment for this "stripped book."

Recycling programs
for this product may
not exist in your area.

ISBN-13: 978-0-373-06030-6

A Dangerous Taste of Passion

First North American Publication 2016

Copyright © 2016 by Anne Mather

All rights reserved. Except for use in any review, the reproduction or utilization of this work in whole or in part in any form by any electronic, mechanical or other means, now known or hereinafter invented, including xerography, photocopying and recording, or in any information storage or retrieval system, is forbidden without the written permission of the publisher, Harlequin Enterprises Limited, 225 Duncan Mill Road, Don Mills, Ontario M3B 3K9, Canada.

This is a work of fiction. Names, characters, places and incidents are either the product of the author's imagination or are used fictitiously, and any resemblance to actual persons, living or dead, business establishments, events or locales is entirely coincidental.

This edition published by arrangement with Harlequin Books S.A.

For questions and comments about the quality of this book, please contact us at CustomerService@Harlequin.com.

® and TM are trademarks of Harlequin Enterprises Limited or its corporate affiliates. Trademarks indicated with ® are registered in the United States Patent and Trademark Office, the Canadian Intellectual Property Office and in other countries.

Printed in U.S.A.

www.Harlequin.com

A DANGEROUS TASTE
OF PASSION

To Kate, the best daughter ever. With all my love.

CHAPTER ONE

HE WAS STANDING on the cliff that rose steeply at the end of the cove.

Was he watching her? Lily didn't know. But she didn't need her intuition to realise who he was. Dee-Dee had told her; had warned her actually. And Dee-Dee seemed to know everything.

But then, Dee-Dee also claimed she had the sight, and no one on the small Caribbean island of Orchid Cay would argue with her. And it was true, the old woman had foretold Lily's mother's illness, and last season's hurricane that had almost destroyed the marina in town.

Lily's father didn't agree that Dee-Dee knew everything. He regarded their housekeeper's visions as just mumbo-jumbo. But Lily supposed that as an Anglican priest he couldn't be seen to have anything to do with the 'black magic' he declared Dee-Dee's claims to be.

Still, right now, Lily was less concerned with Dee-Dee's abilities than with her desire for the man to go away. She didn't like thinking he was watching her and she wondered again what he was doing on the island.

According to Dee-Dee, his name was Raphael Oliveira and he was from New York. The old housekeeper had speculated that he'd got in trouble in the city and had bought one of the most expensive properties on the island to escape from justice.

But even Dee-Dee's speculations couldn't always be relied upon and no one had even known that the house at Orchid Point was for sale.

Whatever, Lily wished he would just turn around and go away. This was the time she usually took her evening swim, but she had no intention of taking her clothes off in front of him—even if he was more than a hundred feet away.

Folding her towel over her arm, she started back towards the rectory. She only permitted herself a surreptitious glance in his direction when she was almost home.

And discovered, to her chagrin, that he was gone.

A week later, Lily was sitting at her desk, entering the details of the previous season's charters into the computer, when someone came into the agency.

She'd worked for Cartagena Charters ever since she'd left the university she'd attended in Florida. It wasn't a particularly demanding job, but Orchid Cay was a small town and there weren't that many jobs that her father would approve of.

Her working area, such as it was, was behind a

screen that separated the counter from the office. Usually her boss, Ray Myers, attended to all enquiries himself. But today Ray was away in Miami, taking delivery of a new two-masted schooner. He'd told Lily there probably wouldn't be any new customers until the weekend, but she was nominally in charge.

Sighing, as much at being interrupted as at the prospect of having to deal with an enquiry herself, Lily slid out of her seat and rounded the Perspex screen into the business area.

A man was there, standing with his back to her, staring out of the plate glass windows at the masts of yachts bobbing in the marina beyond.

He was tall and very tanned, with overly long dark hair, broad shoulders encased in a leather jacket. His thumbs were pushed into the back pockets of tight-fitting jeans, accentuating the fact that they clung to narrow hips and long powerful legs.

Lily swallowed. She knew who he was instantly; had sensed it, she realised, before she'd actually walked round the screen and seen him. It was the same man who'd watched her from the cliff a week ago, the man Dee-Dee had warned her might be dangerous to know.

He'd heard her footsteps and turned almost before she'd had a chance to school her expression. She saw dark brown eyes, long-lashed, above hollow cheekbones, a prominent nose and a thin, yet sensual mouth. Not handsome, she thought, but endlessly fascinating. For the first time she allowed the thought that Dee-Dee might just be right.

'Hi,' he said, his voice as rich and dark as black coffee. If he recognised her, he gave no sign of it. 'Is Myers about?'

Lily hesitated. So he knew Ray, she thought. She hadn't sensed that. Although he spoke in English, he had a faint but distinct accent, as if it wasn't his first language.

'Um… Mr Myers isn't here,' she said, realising he was waiting for an answer. 'Are you a friend of his?'

Oliveira looked as if he doubted the innocence of that question, but he didn't take her up on it. 'Not a friend,' he said. 'But we are acquainted. My name is Rafe Oliveira. He would remember me, I think.'

Lily thought that as far as she was concerned he was virtually unforgettable, but of course she didn't say that. Did he know of his notoriety amongst the island's inhabitants?

And he called himself *Rafe*, she mused, liking it better than Raphael.

Shaking her head at her thoughts, she said, 'Well, I'm afraid Mr Myers is in Miami at present.' Then, subconsciously checking the fact that the hem of her vest had pulled free of her shorts as she got up, she added quickly, 'Can I help you?'

The man regarded her and Lily was instantly aware that the precarious knot she'd made of her tawny hair that morning was beginning to tumble about her ears. Add to that the fact that she was wearing little make-up, and she probably looked hot and bothered.

What an image!

'I think not,' Oliveira said now, lifting his shoulders in a gesture of dismissal, and once again Lily was struck by his harsh attraction.

Though it was not something she wished to dwell on. Her father would have kittens if he thought she was entertaining such thoughts about a man who had created such a stir amongst the island's population.

'When will Myers be back?'

His words interrupted her musings, and Lily arched brows that were several shades darker than her hair. He'd called Ray 'Myers' again, she thought. Which was hardly friendly. Maybe even assuming Ray was an acquaintance was pushing it.

His eyes had drifted towards the marina again and, taking the opportunity to tug her vest down over the wedge of tanned skin she'd exposed, Lily said, 'He should be back the day after tomorrow. Can I give him a message?'

The night-dark eyes turned back in her direction and she was suddenly sure he'd noticed her efforts to cover herself. Not because she could read his mind, however, but because of the faintly mocking expression that had taken the place of his earlier detachment.

'No importa,' he said and, although the words were anything but sensual, she felt an unfamiliar quiver in her stomach. 'It does not matter,' he continued. 'I will speak to him myself when he returns.'

'Okay.'

Lily expected he would go then, but instead he wandered over to the display of leaflets and brochures advertising the many activities—sailing, fishing, scuba-diving—available to visitors.

Flicking through the leaflets with a careless finger, he glanced back at her out of the corners of his eyes. 'Did you enjoy your swim the other evening?' he asked, bringing a surge of bright colour into her face.

From his attitude earlier, she'd begun to believe he couldn't have recognised her from that distance away. She'd never dreamt that he might refer to the fact that he'd seen her, or that he'd guessed what she'd planned to do before he'd appeared.

Had he seen her on the beach before?

Licking her dry lips, she said stiffly, 'I don't know what you're talking about, *señor.*' And if her tone was tight and unfriendly, so what? 'It's some time since I took a swim in the evening.'

Abandoning any pretence of looking at the brochures, he strolled back to the counter, surveying her with a faintly amused gaze. 'You object to my question?' he queried lightly, making her painfully aware that he had no trouble in reading her at all.

'Why should I?' she retorted shortly, realising he was unlikely to believe her. 'Now, is there anything else, *señor*? Because, if not, I have work to do.'

'So conscientious,' he remarked softly, lifting a hand to rake long fingers through the wind-tumbled darkness of his hair. The gesture caused a crease to form in the sleeve of his jacket, and she found herself wondering if the leather felt as soft as it looked.

Unlike the arm underneath, she thought, which she was sure would be taut and corded with muscle.

But such thoughts were not conducive to lowering her blood pressure. The air in the room felt suddenly thicker and Lily folded her arms, as if by doing so she could protect herself from his disturbing presence.

Why didn't he go? she wondered. His business was finished here. Did it amuse him to make fun of her? And why, when he was so obviously out of her league, did her stomach keep tying itself in knots?

'I think I have embarrassed you,' he said, ignoring her very obvious desire for him to leave. 'I did not mean to spy on you.'

Lily's lips parted. 'You've been spying on me?' she exclaimed, as if she'd only just become aware of it, but his mouth compressed at her words.

'You saw me on the cliffs the other evening,' he told her flatly. 'As I saw you. I have not yet acquired the ability to go about the island unseen. I assume that was why you changed your mind about going into the water. I am not a fool, Ms—' He shrugged. 'Ms Fielding, is it not? Your father is the local priest, *no*?'

Lily was taken aback. She hadn't realised he might know her name. But it annoyed her that she cared. Dammit, he wasn't the first man who'd shown her any attention.

'All right,' she said, deciding there was no point in denying it. 'I saw you.' And then, because she didn't see why he should have it all his own way, she added, 'Were you disappointed when I changed my mind?'

She knew she'd startled him. Dear heaven, she'd startled herself. Though startled wasn't quite the word. She was shocked, stunned, gobsmacked at her own audacity. She'd never have believed she could say such a thing.

Predictably, Oliveira recovered first. But that was to be expected, she thought resentfully. He'd probably encountered every kind of provocation in his—what?—maybe almost forty years. A faint smile touched the corners of his mouth, but when he spoke his voice was gentle. *'Sí,'* he said evenly. 'But I was only disappointed to have invaded your privacy.' He paused and then went on, 'You prefer to be alone, *no*?' His smile widened and Lily felt as if every bone in her body was melting. 'Yet there was something…distinctly pagan…about a young woman behaving in such a reckless way.' He arched a dark brow. 'Am I forgiven?'

Lily's mouth was dry. 'I doubt it,' she mumbled, not knowing what else to say, and he inclined his head before starting for the door.

'No matter,' he said, pushing the door open, allowing a little of the humid air to invade the air-conditioned coolness of the office. Then he turned back, but although Lily tensed all he added was 'Perhaps you'd tell Myers that I called?'

CHAPTER TWO

RAFE DROVE BACK to Orchid Point, cursing the impulse that had made him embarrass the girl.

He only knew who she was because his cook spoke of the girl's father with such derision. But then, Luella, like many of the other inhabitants on the island, paid lip service to the Anglican church while secretly attending other forms of religious ceremonies after dark.

He scowled, annoyed with himself for baiting her. Didn't he have enough complications in his life as it was? An ex-wife who persisted in stalking him; a reputation that was in ruins, despite the fact that all charges had been dropped; and the knowledge that living on Orchid Cay, unless he could find something to occupy him, would soon begin to pall.

He swung the four-by-four round a tight curve where hedges of scarlet hibiscus brushed against the side of the Lexus. Nevertheless, his eyes were irresistibly drawn to the blue-green waters of the ocean, creaming on sands that had been bleached a palest ivory by the tropical sun.

It was beautiful, he thought. He'd missed sights like these while he'd been living in New York. His father still lived in Miami, of course, and he'd visited him fairly regularly. But he'd been so busy building up his business, he'd forgotten all about the simple delights of his childhood in Havana.

That was the excuse his ex-wife had given when he'd discovered she'd been cheating on him. He was never home, Sarah had complained, and she'd been lonely. But their marriage had been a mistake from the start, and he'd certainly not been too distressed when he'd had reason to sue for divorce.

Unfortunately, Sarah had fought him every step of the way. Despite the very generous settlement he'd given her, she'd wanted him to forgive her, to take her back, to move back into their penthouse apartment as if nothing had happened.

But Rafe had considered the loss of the luxurious duplex a small price to pay for his freedom. Even when, some months later, Sarah had bluffed her way into his new home and trashed his bedroom, he hadn't brought any charges against her. He'd believed that sooner or later she'd accept that their relationship was over.

But in the last few months Rafe had realised that wasn't going to happen. He'd been arrested for drug smuggling. And, although he'd never had any dealings with the South American cartel Sarah had accused him of joining, it had meant serious lawyer's bills and a court case that had drained him of any enthusiasm to remain in New York.

The experience had made him think seriously about his life. He was almost forty, and for the past twenty years he'd concentrated all his energies into his work.

That was why, when the opportunity to sell out came, he'd taken it. He'd retained only a nominal interest in the Oliveira Corporation and bought land and property from a man who'd won it playing poker in Las Vegas.

For the next couple of years, however restless he became, he intended to take a break, to do some sailing and fishing, and to generally chill out. He need never work again, but he didn't think he could stand that prospect. Nevertheless, in future, he intended to invest in small enterprises. Like Cartagena Charters, for example.

Rafe drove through the village of Coral Key. His home, a sprawling villa made of coral and limestone, occupied the cliffs overlooking a private sandy cove. Rafe had taken to swimming there most mornings, usually before most of his household was awake.

Perhaps the Fielding girl should follow his example.

The gates to the property swung open at his approach, thanks to the electronic pad Steve Bellamy, his butler-cum-assistant, had installed in the car.

As well as vetting all visitors, the ex-policeman acted as chauffeur, computer programmer, and gourmet chef, if required to do so. Though this was a skill he'd sworn Rafe never to divulge to any of his erstwhile colleagues on the New York force.

Rafe parked the Lexus in one bay of the six-car garage and, leaving the keys in the ignition, he strolled around to the back of the villa.

A swimming pool lay basking in the noonday sun and, on either side of the pool, tubs of hibiscus and fragrant oleander tumbled exotically onto the painted tiles. Beneath a striped awning, a teak table was already laid for lunch. Just in case he should choose to eat outdoors.

His housekeeper appeared as he was standing gazing out towards the ocean. Carla Samuels had worked for him for over fifteen years, since long before the breakdown of his marriage. And, although his ex-wife had threatened her with all manner of retribution, she'd insisted on going with Rafe when he'd moved out of the apartment and ultimately to Orchid Cay.

'What time will you be wanting lunch, Mr Oliveira?' she asked, and Rafe turned to her with a lazy shrug.

'I cannot say I am particularly hungry, Carla,' he confessed ruefully. 'Maybe later, hmm?'

'A man needs to eat,' insisted Carla staunchly. 'Wouldn't you like a delicious fillet of grouper, cooked simply with a little butter and lemon?' And when this aroused no apparent interest, 'Or a salad? Luella has got some shellfish, fresh off the boat this morning.' She touched her fingers to her lips. 'You would love them.'

Rafe grinned, sliding his arms out of his jacket and hooking it over one shoulder. 'You don't give up, do you, Carla?' He strolled towards her. 'Okay. I'll have a salad. But tell Luella no mayonnaise, *me oye*?'

Carla's response was indicative of what she thought of his decision. But, apart from checking with him whether he wanted to eat outdoors or in, she'd learned to keep her opinions to herself.

'Outdoors, I think,' Rafe decided, following her into the house. He grimaced. 'God, it's cold in here!'

Carla shrugged. 'Mr Bellamy likes it that way,' she said smugly, hurrying away before her employer could take her up on it.

Rafe tossed his jacket onto a chair in the glass-walled entry and then walked on into a huge reception hall. The floor was Italian-tiled, with a central table overflowing with orchids and lilies. Beyond, a curving stone staircase led to the upper gallery, where all the main bedroom suites were situated.

Rafe's study was in the wing to his left. He was heading in that direction when Steve's voice arrested him. 'Hey, Mr Oliveira,' he called, striding towards Rafe from the direction of the kitchen. 'Got a minute?'

Rafe gave a resigned gesture, turning to rest his shoulders against one of the stone columns that supported the ceiling. 'Do I have a choice?'

Steve pulled a wry face. A tall, well-built man, a

few years older than his employer, he had the kind of face that Rafe thought anyone would trust. 'You always have a choice,' he said now, rumpling his greying hair. 'I only wanted to tell you, you had a visitor while you were in town.'

Rafe surveyed the man curiously. He'd known Bellamy for over two years now, and he knew he wasn't the kind of guy to get upset over nothing. 'A visitor?' he said, frowning at Steve's doubtful expression. 'Grant Mathews, *no*?'

'Close. But I get the feeling Mr Mathews is still licking his wounds from his trip to Las Vegas. I did hear he is short of cash.'

'Men like Mathews are not short of cash for long, Steve,' retorted Rafe flatly. 'Having a cash-flow problem is their usual excuse. You will see, in about six months he will be desperate to buy this house and the land back again.'

Steve's brows rose. 'And will you let him?'

Rafe shrugged. 'That depends.'

'Depends on what?'

'On whether I like living here,' replied Rafe carelessly. 'Do not get too comfortable, Steve. I may find island life is not for me.'

Steve stared at him hard, as if he was trying to see if his employer was serious, but Rafe was getting impatient. 'The visitor,' he prompted, causing the older man to do a double-take. 'You said we had had a visitor. If it was not Grant Mathews, who was it?'

'His daughter,' said Steve at once, and Rafe stared

at him now, trying to come to terms with what he'd heard.

'His daughter?' he echoed. 'I didn't know he had a daughter. What's her name? How old is she?'

'Does that matter?' Steve's tone was dry. 'In her twenties, I'd guess. Her name's Laura. Apparently she and her mother used to live on the island—in this house actually—until her mother remarried and Laura went away to college.'

'I see.' Rafe contemplated what he'd heard. 'Did she say what she wanted?'

'No.' Steve was laconic. 'But she insisted it was you she needed to see.' He paused. 'My opinion is that she's come here hoping to see what you were like. Maybe her father sent her. Maybe not. She certainly seemed interested in you.'

Amusement tugged at the corners of Rafe's mouth. 'Did she now?'

Steve looked disgusted. 'I'd have thought you'd have had enough of women who use their good looks as a weapon,' he retorted shortly, and Rafe gave a sigh.

'Oh, I have,' he agreed flatly, patting the other man on his shoulder. 'And thanks for the heads-up, Steve. I may just be unavailable—again—if Ms Mathews returns, *no*?'

Lily didn't see Rafe Oliveira again for several days.

Ray Myers returned from his trip to Miami and was somewhat ambivalent about the news that a Señor Oliveira had been looking for him.

'How well do you know him?' asked Lily, defending her curiosity on the grounds that she'd worked for Ray for a few years and usually shared his confidence.

Indeed, it was only six months since he'd offered her a chance to invest in the business. The fact that she didn't have that kind of money hadn't soured their relationship. At least, she didn't think it had.

'We've met,' said Ray carelessly now, sitting down at the computer and attempting to turn up the database detailing any charters that had come in since he'd been away. 'I see the *Ariadne* got back okay.'

'Why wouldn't it?' Lily was offhand, but she was hurt that Ray was shutting her out. 'Oh, and by the way, Dave says the engines in the *Santa Lucia* need overhauling. If you want him to do it, you'd better give him a ring.'

Ray glanced up at her. 'I will. Maybe in the next couple of weeks.'

'You might have to take the *Lucia* out of service before then. We've got a group—'

'Oh, yeah, yeah.' Ray interrupted her as his memory kicked in. 'You mean that fishing party from Boston.' He shrugged. 'I wonder if we can get away with leaving it until after their booking. What do you think?'

Lily shrugged without answering him. At any other time she'd have given her opinion, but it wasn't her responsibility, after all. If Ray chose to take chances with his licence, that was his affair. But she couldn't help thinking that in his place she'd have taken the safer option.

Ray scowled, but then, evidently deciding it would be wise not to push it, he said, 'I suppose you know Laura Mathews is back on the island?'

'Laura?' Lily was surprised.

Laura Mathews had been a close friend before they'd each gone their separate ways: Laura to New York, to work in an advertising agency, and Lily to university in Florida.

'No, I haven't heard from her.'

Of course, recently there'd been talk about Laura's father losing a lot of money at the tables in Las Vegas. Once the richest man on Orchid Cay, these days Dee-Dee said he was struggling to survive due to the downturn in the market. And it was rumoured that he was only living there on borrowed time.

Certainly he'd had to sell some property. As witness, the house at Orchid Point, Lily mused with some reluctance.

Years ago, Laura and her mother had lived in the villa that Rafe Oliveira now owned. Laura's parents had separated when she was a child, and since then Grant Mathews had occupied the plantation house alone.

Ray shrugged. 'I heard she's been back a few days,' he said, and Lily gave a shrug.

'Perhaps she's come back to comfort her father,' she remarked casually. Although her memory of the other girl said the opposite.

'Anyway, get on to Dave Tapply and tell him I'd like the *Lucia*'s engines overhauled, but not until after next week,' Ray said now. Then, getting tired of trying to find the information he was looking for, he got up from Lily's desk. 'Print me out a copy of the current financial statement, would you? I'm no good with computers.'

Lily felt a twinge of apprehension. It was only intuition, but Ray wasn't skilled at hiding his feelings and it was apparent that he had more than the *Lucia*'s problems on his mind.

'You look...worried,' she said, despite her determination not to get involved. 'We're not in trouble, are we?'

'You're not,' said Ray at once. 'You had more sense than to invest your hard-earned cash with a crock like me.'

Lily gasped. 'I didn't have any money to invest,' she protested.

'Nor do I,' said Ray dourly. 'Ain't that a shame?'

Lily stared at him. 'But Cartagena Charters is the best on the island.'

'Which isn't saying a lot in the present climate, if you'll forgive the pun. People aren't coming to the island in the off-season like they used to.'

'Some are.'

'The stalwarts, yeah.' Ray was phlegmatic. 'But all these hurricanes in the Caribbean; they're bad for business. You know we've had a couple of cancellations, and since I lost those two boats in that storm last fall it's been a struggle to—dare I say it?—keep my head above water.'

'But they were insured. The boats, I mean.'

'Were they?' Ray gave a mirthless laugh. 'In the small print I think you'll find there was something about excluding acts of God.

'And that's what hurricanes are, Lily. You ask the Reverend, your father. I haven't been able to find an insurer yet who's prepared to accept liability for storms!'

Lily realised the apprehension she'd been feeling earlier had been justified. 'But why buy a new schooner? Can we afford it?'

Ray regarded her warily. 'Does it matter? We needed it,' he reminded her. 'Haven't I just said we lost two boats last fall?'

'Yes.' Lily looked thoughtful. 'And I suppose if you're going to get anyone interested in Cartagena Charters, you have to present a successful front.'

Ray made an affirmative gesture. 'Now you're talking.'

An investor like Rafe Oliveira, thought Lily uneasily. Her nerves prickled at the memory of the other man standing in the office, regarding her with those night-dark eyes.

Oh, God! She swallowed. Was Ray really hoping to get Oliveira interested in the agency? She doubted if even Dee-Dee could foresee what the South American might do if that happened.

Or herself, for that matter.

CHAPTER THREE

LILY WAS TEMPTED to go for a swim that evening.

The prospect of feeling the soft water cooling her overheated body was so appealing after more than a week of avoiding the beach that she couldn't resist.

Ironically, Dee-Dee had also mentioned Laura Mathews as soon as Lily got home from work that afternoon. Little gossip escaped her notice and anything to do with the Mathews family was worthy of a mention.

The West Indian housekeeper usually stayed to provide the Reverend's lunch and prepare the evening meal for both of them. Most afternoons she was still there when Lily got home.

The news about the Mathewses warranted a longer discussion however. Apparently, the gossip was that Laura had been keeping her arrival under wraps. For some reason, no one had previously had an inkling that she was staying at the plantation.

But the news was out now. And, according to Dee-Dee, it was believed that Laura had lost her job in New York. Which might account for the low profile she'd been keeping since she got back. As far as Lily was concerned, she was sorry if things were not going well for the girl. Okay, Laura hadn't had much time for Lily in recent years, but that didn't mean she wished her ill.

Whatever, Lily put these thoughts aside as she dropped her clothes and towel on the sand and splashed into the ocean. It was almost completely dark and there was little chance of her being observed.

Not that there'd been any sign of anyone on the cliffs recently. If there had been, she'd have abandoned her plans.

She could hear the sound of drums in the distance and, knowing what it meant, a shiver ran down her spine. Her father wouldn't be pleased if he learned that his daughter was swimming after dark just yards from the old slave cabins. He didn't even approve of her swimming alone in daylight, and in all honesty Lily usually did what he said.

They'd lived together too long, she thought. Since her mother died when she was in her teens, William Fielding had become infinitely narrower in his outlook. He spent his time writing long boring sermons for his small congregation, and threatening Lily with all manner of retribution if she ignored his words.

Lily had put on a blouse and skirt for supper. Underneath, she'd put on her bikini briefs instead of panties. If her father had asked if she was going out, she wouldn't have lied to him. Perhaps she'd have said she was going for a walk, which was only stretching the truth a little.

And she was twenty-four, after all.

The water felt cool at this time of the evening. It was because the sun had set and there was no heat in the moon's pale light. Yet, glinting on the water, it had its own beauty, a mystical appeal that evoked romantic images of a man and woman making love.

Not that she'd had a lot of experience in that area. A couple of clumsy couplings while she was at university, and a brief affair with her father's curate, had pretty well cured her of casual sex.

Dee-Dee had assured her that with the right partner it could be wonderful. But then, Dee-Dee wanted her to attend one of the ceremonies that sometimes took place and see what she was missing for herself.

So far Lily had resisted her efforts. Not that she wasn't curious, because she was. She wondered if Rafe Oliveira had had any experience of black magic. Though why she should associate those thoughts with him after only one encounter was rather more disturbing.

Turning onto her back, she gazed up at the arc of stars above her head and let his dark face fill her vision. It wasn't difficult. She'd been thinking about him off and on for days.

But the sudden quiver in her belly, the sensation of liquidity between her legs was different. So different that she found herself suddenly short of breath.

What was happening to her? With a tentative hand, she explored the source of her feelings, shivering with an ache that had nothing to do with the temperature of the water. She felt weak, trembly, totally unlike her normal self.

Dear God, was this what Dee-Dee had been talking about? Would sex with a man like Oliveira be everything the old woman had said and more?

She tried to relax. She didn't have that much longer before her father would start wondering where she was. And it was such a beautiful evening. A night for lovers, she thought, allowing her hand to stray over her stomach to the tight buds of her nipples.

And then she caught her breath in alarm. Someone was there, standing in the shadow of a clump of palm trees that grew at the edge of the dunes. It was a man; she was sure of it. And another image of Rafe Oliveira flashed before her eyes. Immediately, she turned onto her stomach and gazed fiercely into the darkness. But, although she stared until her eyes ached with the effort, the shadows, when they eventually shifted, revealed nothing but the trees.

She frowned. Could she have imagined it? She was tired, and in the darkness it was easy to create shapes in the gloom. But the warnings she'd been given came back to haunt her and she swam quickly back to the shore.

The idea that what she might have seen had been less substantial than a human being didn't reassure her. Dee-Dee's talk of black magic, the distant sound of the drums, were too real to be ignored. As for the souls of the walking dead… Lily shivered again. It was all too easy to be spooked by such tales.

Deciding she'd spent too long in the water, Lily walked bravely up onto the beach. She towelled herself dry more urgently than usual and then quickly dressed in the skimpy cap-sleeved blouse and pleated skirt.

The blouse was made of amber lace, and clung to her still-damp breasts and shoulders. But although her skirt was shorter than normal and provocatively flared, it was less revealing. She hesitated before peeling off the bikini briefs. But who was going to see her now? There was no dark figure on the cliffs to watch her and, with a slightly jerky movement, she stripped them off.

She didn't like to think what her father would say if he could see her. Yet what had she done, after all? Swum after dark—albeit topless—without his permission? Taken off her wet briefs so her legs would dry.

It wasn't anything any other girl her age might have done, she assured herself. However strictly he treated her, she needed some freedom. And he needed to remember she wasn't a child.

Lily had reached the modest rectory before she saw the vehicle parked to one side of the building. It was a large four-by-four, and it was unfamiliar to her.

Which made her apprehensive. She'd have thought she'd recognise any automobile that might turn up at her father's door. After the feelings she'd had while she was taking her swim, it was worrying. If they had visitors, then Reverend Fielding was unlikely to be holed up in his study as she'd anticipated.

Before she could formulate any plan as to how she was going to get into the house without being seen, a man stepped out of the shadows to confront her.

'*Buenas noches*, Ms Fielding,' he said with suave politeness. 'Are you well?'

Rafe Oliveira!

Lily was instantly conscious of the amber lace clinging to her breasts like a second skin and the embarrassing knowledge that, whether he knew it or not, she was naked under her skirt. The pleasant draught of cool air that had fanned her thighs as she walked up the beach was now banished by the rush of heat that spread down from her stomach. And an insistent pulse made itself felt between her legs.

Because of this, because she felt so damnably vulnerable, her response was uncharacteristically sharp.

'Have you been spying on me again, Señor Oliveira?' she demanded, not caring right then whether the accusation was justified or not.

The veranda behind them was lit by hanging lanterns and in their muted light she saw the way his eyebrows rose. His dark eyes registered first surprise, then amusement.

'I have not been spying on you, Ms Fielding,' he said mildly. 'Though I have to admit I think it is most unwise to swim alone at this time of the evening.'

'So you were watching me!'

'No! *Por el amor de Dios*.' He was impatient. 'Your father was worried about you. He said you'd gone for a walk. As he was worried, I offered to look for you. I have just stepped out of the house. And here you are.'

Lily chewed on her lower lip. 'I suppose you guessed I hadn't gone for a walk?'

'I did not give it a great deal of thought,' retorted Rafe not altogether truthfully. But he knew exactly what she meant.

Watching him out of the corner of her eye, Lily didn't know whether to believe him or not. He was wearing black this evening, or some dark colour anyway. It accentuated his disturbing appeal and, despite her irritation, Lily was not immune to it.

'Are you going to tell my father I was lying to him?' she persisted, and Rafe made a careless gesture with his hands.

'Why should I?' he asked indifferently. 'You are not a child, Ms Fielding. If you choose to behave recklessly, that is your…um…funeral, *no*?'

Lily's expression was mutinous. 'So why did you offer to look for me?'

Rafe shook his head. 'I could say I was concerned about you, but in all honesty I was more concerned about the poor *bastardo* who might be arrested as a—what do you say?—a Peeping Tom, *no*?'

Lily held up her head. 'There was no one else around,' she insisted.

'You are sure?'

She wasn't. Remembering her nerves when she'd heard the drums earlier, and her belief that there had been someone hiding in the trees, Lily had no answer to that.

'Well, as you can see, I am safely home,' she said stiffly. 'Don't let us keep you.'

Rafe's teeth ground together in frustration. 'Do you think it is wise to alert your father to your return until you have had time to change?'

'I'm sure Daddy is working in his study. He's probably forgotten all about my absence by now.'

'You think?' Rafe's dark eyes swept down her body. 'Having met Father Fielding—'

'It's the *Reverend* Fielding, actually.'

'Bien.' Rafe allowed himself to be corrected. '*No obstante*, having met *Reverend* Fielding, I would not put my faith in that belief.' He gestured to the house behind him. 'I am of the opinion that he is waiting for us both to return.'

Lily's face flamed. 'Well, so what? He's unlikely to ask what I've been doing while you're here.'

'Possibly not.' Rafe thought he was being extremely patient in the circumstances. 'But, *perdón*, is that not part of your bikini dangling from your fingers? It is, as they say, a dead giveaway, *no*?'

Lily caught her breath. She'd forgotten she was carrying the briefs. And how revealing was that?

Rafe sucked in a breath. 'I assume you are aware there are certain—illegal—activities taking place at this moment in the old slave cabins at the end of the beach.'

Lily suppressed the urge to cross her legs. How did he know what was going on in the old cabins? It increased the possibility that someone else might have been watching her? she thought uneasily.

She shivered. There was something disturbingly intimate about this conversation.

'I... I'd better go and change, *señor*,' she said, deciding she might have misjudged him. But when she attempted to go past him, Rafe stepped into her path.

'You should not take your safety for granted, you know,' he said softly, and Lily suddenly found it difficult to take a breath. He put out his hand and lifted a strand of her wet hair, rubbing its silky texture between his thumb and forefinger. 'It would be very easy for...someone...to take advantage of you.'

Lily swallowed a little convulsively and Rafe's hand fell to his side. Whatever vibes she'd been giving off, he'd evidently thought better of the impulse to touch her.

Which was a shame because, for a heart-stopping moment, she'd wanted him to pull her into his arms.

And how crazy was that?

He stepped back, spreading his hands again in a gesture of acceptance. But when Lily moved to leave, he said softly, 'Please, when next we meet do not address me as *señor*. My name is Rafe.' His lips twisted. 'I wish you would use it.'

The air left Lily's lungs on an uneven breath. Had he sensed what she'd been thinking? It was difficult to know. But one thing was certain—on an island as small as Orchid Cay, the chances of them meeting again were almost unavoidable. And she should remember that.

'I must go,' she said and hurried past him, her flesh tingling uncontrollably at the brush of his taut muscular frame against hers.

He followed her inside, intercepting her father, enabling her to make her escape upstairs. And for that she was grateful. But if he hadn't turned up as he had, her father would probably have been none the wiser.

He was gone by the time she came downstairs again. She'd taken a quick shower and changed into clean shorts and a tee shirt. But her father was standing in the doorway to his study, and one look at his face as he bid her to join him warned her that he expected an explanation.

'Where have you been?' he demanded at once and, although Lily knew he must have been worried about her, she resented his domineering tone. 'You didn't say you were going for a walk on the beach. You've been gone more than an hour!'

Lily pressed her lips together, silencing her indignation. 'I'm sorry.'

'That's not good enough, Lilian.' William Fielding frowned. 'You know how I worry about you.'

'I am sorry.'

Lily didn't know what else to say, but fortunately William Fielding had other things on his mind.

'We've had a visitor,' he said abruptly. 'A Señor Oliveira. From Orchid Point. I would have liked you to meet him.'

'I did meet him,' began Lily, not knowing what Oliveira might have said and determined not to prove herself any more of a liar than she felt already.

But her father wouldn't let her finish. 'I know that,' he interrupted her shortly. 'He offered to go and find you. I don't know what you were thinking, Lily. You must know what goes on at the other end of the beach after dark.'

She was contemplating her response when her father spoke again. 'You've changed your clothes,' he said, having just noticed her damp hair. 'Wasn't it a little late to have a shower?'

'I was hot,' declared Lily, refusing to be provoked. She paused. 'What did Señor Oliveira want? I didn't know you knew him.'

'I didn't until this evening.' William Fielding's brows remained creased. 'I assume he introduced himself to you when he found you.'

Lily sighed. 'Actually, I'd already met him. He came into the agency a few days ago looking for Ray.'

Reverend Fielding frowned. 'I wonder what he wanted with Myers.'

Lily shrugged. 'To hire a boat, maybe.'

'Oh, I think not.' Her father shook his head. 'I'm sure a man like him will have his own yacht.'

Now it was Lily's turn to frown. 'A man like him?' She echoed his words. 'Who is he? What do you know about him?'

'Only what I've read in the newspapers,' replied her father defensively, retiring behind his desk. 'You must have heard he used to run a successful group of companies in New York.' He stared at her, his eyes intent suddenly. 'I can't believe that piece of gossip slipped either yours or Dee-Dee's notice.'

Lily tried to control the warmth that flooded into her throat as he spoke.

'Well, yes,' she admitted. 'But that doesn't explain what he was doing here.'

Her father sank into his leather recliner now, lifting his shoulders dismissively. 'I imagine he wanted to meet me.'

'But why?'

'Does there have to be a reason?' Reverend Fielding looked impatient. 'The man's living on the island, Lily. Perhaps he felt in need of spiritual guidance.'

'And did you give him spiritual guidance?' Lily couldn't hide her scepticism.

'As most of my energies were taken up with finding you, then no, our conversation was correspondingly brief.'

And, as if reminded of her transgressions, her father's scowl deepened. 'But I will not be made to feel guilty when we both know you were in the wrong.'

Lily caught her breath. 'I'm not trying to make you feel guilty, Dad.'

'It sounds like it to me. Trying to shift the blame, at the very least.'

Lily shook her head. 'I just don't understand why that man would come to see you. You're an Anglican minister. He's Spanish. He must be a Catholic.'

'Dee-Dee supports another religion entirely, but she comes to my church on Sundays,' declared her father, showing he wasn't half as ignorant of what was going on as she'd imagined. 'Has it occurred to you that his own church may have let him down?'

Lily blinked. 'Let him down, how?'

'Well…' Her father looked a little reluctant to continue. 'We don't know how it happened, do we?'

'How what happened?' Lily was impatient. 'There is something you're not telling me, isn't there?'

'Only that we shouldn't judge anyone lest we ourselves be judged in return,' replied her father pedantically, resorting to one of his texts instead of giving her a straight answer.

He shuffled the papers on his desk and gave her a nod of approval. 'At least you're home safely, my dear.' He rescued his prayer book from beneath the pile of notes. 'Shall we offer a little prayer of thanks?'

CHAPTER FOUR

'THAT FEMALE IS here again,' said Steve Bellamy, putting his head round the door of Rafe's study after the most perfunctory of knocks. 'Do you want me to deal with her?'

Rafe, who had been examining a nautical map showing all the shoals and reefs present in the waters surrounding the island, looked up with a blank expression. *'Qué?'*

'Laura Mathews,' Steve prompted, coming further into the room. 'Grant Mathews's daughter.' Steve regarded him enquiringly. 'But I see you're busy.'

Rafe met the man's challenging gaze with a slight smile playing about his lips. 'She is very persistent.'

'She is.' Steve shrugged. 'What would you like me to tell her?'

Rafe shook his head. He didn't feel like dealing with a possibly hysterical woman. 'Tell her I've gone sailing,' he said, throwing his pen down on the desk and getting to his feet.

Steve's eyebrows rose. 'But you don't have a sailing vessel at present, Mr Oliveira. Your boat is still moored in Newport.'

'She doesn't know that,' retorted Rafe, refusing to acknowledge why the prospect of looking at sailing craft suddenly filled him with such a feeling of anticipation. 'As far as Ms Mathews is concerned, I will be away for the rest of the day.'

Lily was sitting at her desk, sorting through a pile of invoices to see which needed paying first, when she heard the outer door open. Ray was manning the agency this morning so she didn't bother to leave her seat.

But, hearing Ray's gruff voice interacting with one that was all too familiar, she felt a film of perspiration dampen her upper lip. A thread of moisture trickled down between her breasts and she sucked in a nervous breath. She had hoped it might be some time before Rafe Oliveira came into the agency again.

Shifting a little uncomfortably on her chair, she tried not to listen to their low-voiced exchange. She wasn't interested, she told herself. The reasons for Oliveira being here had nothing to do with her.

Her thighs were sticking to the plastic seat, however, thanks to the cotton shorts she was wearing. She wanted to move, to conceal herself in the restroom but, when she tried getting up, the legs of her chair scraped noisily over the wooden floor.

She almost groaned aloud. Now Oliveira would know she was there, eavesdropping on their conversation. *Spying on him!* Gritting her teeth, she got up and switched on the radio, tuning in to a Southern States reggae station that successfully drowned out any other sound.

She wondered if Oliveira knew Cartagena Charters was in trouble. Obviously Ray had contacted him. That was why he'd come into the agency a week ago. But the notion that he might decide to invest or even become a partner in the firm was something else. It was looking more and more likely that the man did have some interest in the company.

'Lily, have you got a minute?'

Before she could continue with that thought, Ray interrupted her. She had no choice now. She had to show herself.

She paused a moment, examining the open neckline of her shirt, checking that the hem wasn't displaying any revealing wedges of skin. Then, resigning herself in anticipation of Rafe's dark-eyed appraisal, she came round the screen to the front of the agency.

Rafe sensed her reluctance to speak to him again as soon as he saw her. She had her glorious mane of sun-streaked brown hair skewered in a precarious knot this morning and she was wearing a simple white shirt and coffee-coloured shorts.

Nothing glamorous, but she looked stunning even so. And probably didn't realise it.

'Yes?' she said, deliberately not looking in Rafe's direction. 'Did you want something, Ray?'

'Yeah.' Myers glanced at his companion before continuing amiably. 'You've met my assistant, Lily, haven't you, Mr Oliveira?'

Rafe inclined his head as Lily was obliged to acknowledge him. *'Por supuesto,'* he said smoothly. 'It's good to see you again...um... Lily.' The hesitation over her name was deliberate, she was sure.

His slight yet unmistakable accent scraped across her nerves, like sandpaper over raw skin. His dark eyes were surveying her with their usual intentness, making her aware of her shortcomings, making her aware of herself.

She managed a polite smile and then, turning to her employer again, she arched an enquiring brow. 'Is something wrong?'

'Hell, no!' Ray was far too eager to dismiss that idea, in her opinion. 'I want to show Mr Oliveira the layout of the marina, that's all. To show him what a successful business we've got here. Could you delay your lunch break for another—oh, say an hour?'

'Of course.'

Rafe thought there was a trace of doubt in her agreement. But an element of relief, too. What was troubling her? Had she been afraid her employer would ask her to show him around?

But no. It was obvious Myers was intent on trying to usher Rafe out of the door before Lily could say another word.

For his part, Rafe was less inclined to accommodate him. He would have much preferred to talk to Lily. She must know what was really going on with the agency. But she'd evidently not been eager to see him again and he could guess why.

That whole incident about her swimming after dark was obviously still niggling her. Yet all he had been concerned about was her safety.

But did she believe that?

Did he?

'Okay.' Ray grinned at Lily and she concluded he was optimistic about this development. 'After you, Mr Oliveira. If we hustle, we may have time for a beer at Mac's Bar.'

Rafe said nothing. He had no intention of making this a social occasion. But if it pleased Myers to pretend otherwise, then so be it. The guy would find out soon enough.

'*Adios*, Lily,' he said, resisting Myers's attempt to hurry him. '*Hasta luego!*' See you later!

Lily only nodded, but Rafe could see the uncertainty in her eyes. She had cat's eyes, he thought, green and wary. Was part of the struggle she was having an effort not to let Myers down? He suspected she knew more about the business than she was saying.

When the door closed behind them, Lily breathed a sigh of relief. She'd been half afraid that Ray might ask her to accompany them. And how could she remain silent if he started boasting about the agency's success again?

* * *

They were back in less than half an hour.

Lily, who had been expecting them to be at least an hour, felt a surge of curiosity as Rafe Oliveira followed Ray into the agency. Why had they come back? Why hadn't they done as Ray had suggested and continued their conversation in Mac's Bar?

Did Oliveira want to look at the agency's financial statements? It seemed likely. Ray was a fool if he thought he could pull the proverbial wool over the other man's eyes.

But, 'Hey,' Ray greeted her cheerfully enough, though she could tell from his expression that things hadn't gone exactly as he'd planned. 'You can get off now,' he added as Lily got to her feet, and she realised he wanted to discuss his business without a critical audience.

'Okay.'

Lily's eyes flickered over Rafe Oliveira before she scooted into the back to get her bag. Then, with a half-smile that she managed to offer to both of them, she pulled open the door and escaped into the hot humid air of midday.

She usually bought a sandwich and a cappuccino at the nearest coffee shop before finding a quiet spot in Palmetto Park to eat her lunch. With its tree-shaded paths and tropical gardens, the park was a favourite place for picnics.

It adjoined the harbour, and in centuries past had been the holding area for slaves bought by local wealthy landowners. Lily had always thought it was fitting that it had now been turned into an amenity everyone—rich or poor—could enjoy.

She'd walked a little away from the agency and was preparing to cross the street when a hand gripped her arm just above her elbow.

Her initial reaction wasn't one of alarm. She'd lived on Orchid Cay all her life and there were few people among the locals she wasn't familiar with. Yet almost immediately the strength and coolness of those hard fingers had her turning to see who had accosted her, and she wasn't entirely surprised to see Rafe Oliveira's dark face.

'Hi,' he said, releasing her almost at once. 'Can we talk?'

Lily was tempted to say *No* and walk on, but that would have been rude. Besides, she was fairly sure Ray wouldn't like her to offend the man.

'It's my lunch hour,' she said unnecessarily. He had obviously heard what Ray had said earlier. 'If this is to do with the business, I think you ought to speak to Mr Myers.'

Rafe expelled an exasperated breath. 'This has nothing to do with Ray Myers,' he declared shortly. 'I know it is your lunch hour. I heard what was said. That was what I was about to ask you. Will you come and have lunch with me? There are lots of small eating establishments around here.'

Lily assumed a sudden interest in the strap of her bag. But that didn't stop her pulse from racing like a jackhammer. Why was he doing this? Why in God's name would he want to have lunch with her?

'Why me?' she asked at last, voicing her doubts. 'Why not Ray?'

Good question! Rafe regarded her with considering eyes, wondering if he really knew the answer.

'Perhaps I prefer to have lunch with a beautiful young woman,' he said drily. 'Is there a problem?'

'Well, I'm sure Mr Myers expected you to show more interest in the company,' Lily declared stoically. 'You hardly had time to assess the viability of the business before you left.'

Now Rafe's dark brows arched expressively. 'And that is your concern, *si*? You are perhaps a partner in the company?'

Lily felt her face go red. 'I work with Ray, that's all.' She paused. 'But you must have had some reason for coming into the agency again.'

Rafe shrugged. 'And if I did?'

Lily decided to go for broke. 'Well, is it true? Have you decided to take a financial interest in Cartagena Charters?'

'Have lunch with me and you may find out,' said Rafe adroitly, watching the play of emotions that crossed her face.

Lily shook her head. 'I don't think so,' she said. And then, as another thought occurred to her, 'I bet this wasn't Ray's idea.'

'I can understand why you would think that,' he murmured softly. 'You must know he is more interested in hiding the company's failures than in presenting a balanced picture of its assets.' He shrugged. 'But you can tell him he will have to start telling the truth if he expects any further interest from me.'

'Ray just exaggerates a little.' Her tongue sought the roof of her mouth. 'It hasn't been an easy time for him.'

'It has not been an easy time for anyone.' Rafe stifled a curse, glancing about them in some exasperation. 'And do you honestly expect me to continue this conversation here?' He nodded across the street. 'There is a man over there who has been watching me ever since I left the agency. What do you think he is doing, hmm? Propping up the sidewalk? Checking out the talent? I think not.'

Lily couldn't help herself. Ignoring his groan of frustration, she turned to look. And, sure enough, there was a man standing across the street. But whether he was watching them was arguable. Besides, he had a camera hanging from his neck, just like any other tourist.

'You think I'm paranoid, *si*?' Rafe taunted her. 'You do not think that, after all this time, I might not recognise a paparazzo when I see one?' He shook his head. 'So, will you have lunch with me? If not, I—and my escort—will leave you alone.'

Lily's lips parted as once again she gave the man, who did indeed appear to be watching them, another quick appraisal. It occurred to her that it might be herself that he was watching and her skin prickled as it had done that evening on the beach.

'Who is he?'

'I have no idea.' Rafe shrugged. 'He may be working for one of the tabloid newspapers, or perhaps he is DEA, or CIA. I do not care to find out.'

Lily stared at him. 'But why would either the DEA or the CIA be interested in us?'

Rafe pulled a face. 'Evidently you do not read the newspapers. *Dios*, my name was splashed across the headlines for weeks.'

Lily was stunned. She knew the DEA was the United States Drug Enforcement Agency. 'Are you saying you were involved with drugs?'

'*Mierda!* No!' Rafe didn't mince his words. 'But I have no intention of defending myself here. What is your decision?'

Lily hesitated. What she knew she should do was thank him politely for his invitation and walk away.

Yet she couldn't deny she was tempted.

She found herself saying, 'All right. I will have lunch with you.'

If only to find out why he'd gone to see her father, she reassured herself staunchly. Not because just looking at him caused a funny feeling in her stomach.

'*Bien.*'

Without any further hesitation, Rafe took her arm and steered her along the street.

However, Lily pulled away as soon as she was able

and said tersely, 'But I'd prefer not to eat in a restaurant. I usually have a sandwich in Palmetto Park.'

'And you are suggesting I should do the same?' he queried incredulously, and Lily caught her breath.

In khaki cargo pants and a black tee shirt, he looked lean and dark—and dangerous, she thought, her skin prickling again. Was she really thinking of getting involved with this man?

'That's up to you,' she said now, half hoping he would refuse.

But he didn't. 'Very well,' he agreed with a swift glance over his shoulder. 'You had better tell me where we find this—*picnic*—lunch.'

Lily started to respond and then, out of the corner of her eye, she saw the man he had spoken of earlier. He was standing, half hidden by the bole of a palm tree, just a dozen yards away.

'We...we're still being observed,' she said abruptly, realising she hadn't quite believed him before. 'That man—the one you mentioned. He's over there.'

Rafe knew a momentary twinge of impatience. It crossed his mind that he shouldn't involve her in his affairs. She was too young, for one thing. And did he seriously want another female's feelings on his conscience?

'I did warn you,' he said now, giving the man a passing glance. 'So perhaps lunch is off, *si*? We should just agree to go our own separate ways.'

Lily hesitated. 'Um...not necessarily,' she heard herself say with some amazement. Why, when she'd been having such doubts about her involvement with him, wasn't she seizing this chance to get away?

But then, Oliveira had said he might tell her what was going on with Ray, she defended herself fiercely. Taking a breath, she added, 'That is, if you're still willing to join me in the park.'

CHAPTER FIVE

THE COFFEE SHOP where Lily usually bought herself a sandwich and a polystyrene mug of cappuccino was on the other side of the street.

Breaking free of her escort, Lily started to cross the road. Only to halt in alarm when Rafe grabbed her arm again and dragged her back.

Out of the path of a speeding minibus that had showed no intention of stopping.

She heard Rafe's angry words in her ear, his hot breath against the nape of her neck and found she was trembling. She was sure his words were not repeatable, but fortunately she couldn't understand them.

She didn't think he was speaking to her, however, and she turned to him with a breathless word of gratitude.

'*Idiota,*' he muttered, after she had stopped shaking. 'He could have killed you.'

'But he didn't,' said Lily, grateful for his vigilance. 'I don't know how to thank you. What I did was stupid. I should have looked both ways.'

'*Sí,*' he agreed, his face still dark with concern. 'But that—that maniac was not about to stop.'

Rafe grimaced and then, realising she needed reassurance, his expression cleared. 'It would be such a waste to lose you,' he added with gentle sensuality. 'Myers would be devastated, I am sure, and the good *padre*, your father, would never forgive me.'

The way he was looking at her caused all the oxygen to drain from Lily's lungs. Although he was no longer touching her, she felt breathless, weak. She kept telling herself it was the result of the near-accident, but she couldn't look away from his disturbing gaze.

What was there about those hollow cheekbones and that thin-lipped mouth that caused such a visceral reaction inside her? she asked herself incredulously. Why, when she knew she wouldn't like to make an enemy of this man, was she allowing herself to get involved with him?

'I think perhaps I should go back to the agency,' she said now, her voice still a little uneven, but Rafe only arched a mocking brow.

'You disappoint me,' he said. 'I was looking forward to spending more time with you.'

Lily sighed uncertainly. But it would have seemed churlish to abandon him after he'd virtually saved her life, she thought defensively.

'All right,' she said, looking up and down the street again before adding, 'The place where I buy my sandwiches is across the road. If you are certain you want to have lunch with me, we should join the queue.'

The queue?

Rafe scowled as he saw that there was indeed a queue of people waiting outside the coffee shop across the street. And, in the present circumstances, he had no desire to spend the next fifteen minutes waiting in line to buy a greasy burger and an indifferent cup of coffee.

'Are you sure you would not rather find a small eatery and sit down?' he asked, aware that, for all her defiant courage, she still looked rather pale.

'Humour me,' he went on, aware that her eyes had been drawn to the open neckline of his shirt. The brown column of his throat seemed to intrigue her and he was impatiently aware of his own reaction to her. Running a hand over the triangle of dark hair exposed by his shirt, he said roughly, 'I had quite a shock, too.'

Lily hesitated. There was no doubt that the idea of standing in a queue for several minutes before then searching for an empty bench in the park was daunting.

Besides, the man with the camera was still watching them and, as she glanced his way, she saw him raise the camera towards them. 'All right,' she said quickly, expelling an uneasy sigh. 'Not least because I don't like anyone taking my picture without my permission.'

* * *

The eating place Rafe chose was not somewhere Lily had ever been before. Which was a relief. Not that she thought anyone would recognise her with Rafe Oliveira, the man who had left New York apparently under a cloud, and who now owned the exclusive villa at Orchid Point.

For his part, whether the proprietor had recognised him or not, they were given a table inside. Thankfully, they were away from the windows, away from the humidity that had already caused a sheen of sweat to dampen Rafe's spine.

Or was that his unwilling reaction to the near-accident? Had his stalker taken a picture of that? Whatever, it was frustrating to know that even here, on this exotic island, he couldn't escape from his past.

But wasn't he just encouraging more gossip by inviting Lily to have lunch with him? What was there about her that caused him to break the habits of a lifetime? He'd never behaved so recklessly before; never felt so attracted to a woman—a girl, really—who was so totally different from the women he'd known.

Lily refused the wine she was offered and accepted a lime juice spritzer instead. It was a speciality of the island, a mixture of fresh lime juice and soda water. Served over ice in a tall glass, it was the perfect drink for a hot day.

Rafe ordered a beer and then they both chose the seafood salad. Served with warm rolls and a choice of mayonnaise, it was delicious. Much better than the chicken salad sandwich she'd been planning to buy, Lily had to admit.

When they'd been served, Lily met Rafe's dark eyes with a rueful gaze. 'This is nice,' she said, feeling she had to show her gratitude. 'And I do feel much better now.'

'That is good.' Rafe lifted his glass of beer and regarded her over the rim. 'It could have ended so much differently.'

'Well, I could have been knocked down by that minibus,' she agreed fervently. 'You saved my life.'

'What I really meant was that our picture might have appeared in the local newspaper, *no*?' Rafe remarked drily. 'I do not think Father—*Reverend*—Fielding would have approved of that.'

Lily was sure he wouldn't. Her father would be bound to think the worst. She bit her lip. 'You don't think the photographer would follow us here?'

'He might,' said Rafe thoughtfully. 'But I can assure you he will not come into the restaurant.' Rafe grimaced. 'That would entail spending money that they are not being paid.'

Lily shook her head. 'Don't you mind?'

Rafe groaned. 'Of course I mind,' he responded wearily. 'But I am used to it. And, hopefully, sooner or later he will realise he is wasting his time following me and find some other poor fool to hound.'

'How did he know where you lived?' Lily asked without thinking, and then knew a moment's embarrassment at her own audacity. 'I mean,' she murmured uncomfortably, 'why is he still interested in you?'

'Because I am so *un*interesting, *si*?' Rafe teased her mockingly, but this time Lily didn't take the bait.

'I shouldn't have asked,' she said ruefully. 'It's really nothing to do with me.' She paused and then, changing the subject, 'This salad is delicious, isn't it?'

'Oh, Lily!' Rafe sighed. 'Do not look at me like that. You can ask me anything—within reason. As for why I am of such interest to the paparazzi, I fear my ex-wife is to blame.'

Lily stared at him. 'Your ex-wife?'

'Yes. You did not know I had been married?'

'I know nothing about you, *señor*,' she replied, her breath quickening a little. That was not absolutely true but he didn't need to know that.

'Well, I was married. For a few short and—dare I say—unhappy years?' He shrugged. 'And please, I wish you would call me Rafe. Or I shall have to call you Ms Fielding, *no*?'

Lily lifted a crusty roll and bit into it thoughtfully. 'I still don't understand—' she began, and then broke off when she realised she was being nosy again.

'Sarah—my ex-wife—was responsible for me being arrested on drug charges in the first place,' Rafe told her, guessing what her question had been going to be. 'When we separated, she swore she would get back at me. And she did.'

Lily's lips parted. 'But that's awful!'

'I fear it is human nature,' said Rafe, raising his beer to his lips again. He emptied the glass and then summoned the waiter before nodding towards Lily's half-empty tumbler. 'Would you like another of those?'

'Oh—no, thank you.'

Lily shook her head, wondering if it was only her imagination, or were the other occupants of the café staring at them now? Perhaps it was just the peremptory way Rafe had summoned the waiter. Whatever, she tried to ignore them and concentrate on her meal.

There was silence for a few moments and then Rafe spoke again. 'Your father is an interesting man, is he not?'

Lily blinked. Although earlier she'd been curious to know what the two men had spoken about, other things had distracted her.

'If…if you say so,' she murmured, casting a surreptitious glance at the waiter who had brought him another beer. She bit her lip. 'Thank you for not telling him where I was when you found me the other evening.'

'I told him that you were on your way back to the rectory when I encountered you,' declared Rafe carelessly. 'Was that not the truth?'

Lily hesitated. 'Well, yes. But, like you, he would not have approved of me swimming alone.'

Rafe shrugged, lifting his beer and resting his free arm on the table. Despite her interest in the conversation, Lily couldn't help noticing how brown his flesh was, taut and muscular, with a scattering of dark hair above the leather strap of a simple Patek Philippe watch.

His fingers were long, his hands large and capable. Despite what she knew of him—and that mostly from Dee-Dee—he did not look as if he'd spent all his time behind a desk. Those hands were strong and powerful. Without them, she might not be sitting here enjoying her lunch.

A shiver passed down her spine at the memory of his hands against her skin. He had gripped her arm so strongly. She might well have a bruise in the morning. But that was nothing compared to what might have happened if he hadn't acted so quickly.

She suddenly became aware that he was watching her too and, despite her determination not to be disconcerted again, her colour deepened. 'Um…why did you want to see my father?' she asked, desperate to escape the intimacy of his gaze. 'You are not a member of the Anglican church, are you?'

'Hardly.' Rafe's eyes were far too knowing, but he chose to answer her question. 'My parents—my mother is dead, but my father is still alive and lives in Miami—were good Catholics. We lived in Havana until I was about eight years old and—' his lips twisted '—I made my confession regularly, like all the members of my family.'

Lily nodded, more than willing to listen to his attractive voice.

'But, I have to say, these days I do not involve myself in any religion, *pequeña*. Not even the very active sect to whom I believe your housekeeper belongs, *no*?'

Lily arched her brows in surprise. 'How do you know about Dee-Dee?'

Rafe lay back in his chair, cradling his glass between his fingers. 'I too have a housekeeper,' he said easily. 'There is very little that misses Carla's attention, *no*?'

Or yours either, thought Lily, though this time she avoided an unguarded outburst. Then, cautiously, 'You still haven't told me why you wanted to see my father.'

'Did he not tell you himself?'

'Obviously not.' Lily had the impression he was enjoying her curiosity. She lifted her shoulders, refusing to be provoked. 'But if you don't want to tell me, I suppose I ought to be getting back to work.'

Rafe's grin took her by surprise. 'You are annoyed with me, *no*?'

'No.' Lily managed to make a dismissive gesture. 'I wasn't that interested.'

'Ah.' Rafe didn't sound as if he believed her. 'So—talk to me about yourself, *niña*. Do you like your job at the agency?'

'I really ought to be going—'

'Not yet,' said Rafe, leaning across the table to capture the hand she'd rested on the table prior to getting up. 'Tell me, why are you not wearing a ring?' His thumb rubbed sensuously over her finger. 'Or are all the men on Orchid Cay as blind as your employer?'

Lily caught her breath, sure that once again half the eyes in the small restaurant were on them. 'If you mean why am I not married...?' She shrugged. 'I've not yet found anyone I'd like to spend my life with.'

Until now, she thought incredulously. Despite everything she'd heard about Rafe Oliveira, he was still the most fascinating man she'd ever met.

'That is sad.'

Rafe met her gaze for a long disturbing moment, and then dragged his eyes away. What was he doing, flirting with this young woman? This girl, who seemed so naïve in many ways. Cursing himself, he added, 'In Cuba, where I was born, many girls find an *esposo* as soon as they leave school.'

'I used to think that was what my father wanted too,' Lily told him, understanding what he meant, and then felt the colour rise into her cheeks. 'Not that that's of any interest to you.'

'*Al contrario.* Everything about you interests me, *niña.*' Despite himself, Rafe thought wryly, aware of how smooth her skin was beneath his fingers. 'But you have changed your mind, *sí*?'

'Well...' Lily was encouraged to go on. 'He did try to fix me up with Jacob Proctor. His curate,' she explained as Rafe arched an enquiring brow. 'But I think he realised that if I got married and moved to one of the other islands when Jacob got his own parish, I wouldn't be around to care for him.'

Rafe caught his lower lip between his teeth for a moment. Then he said, 'This—this Jacob? You were in love with him?'

Lily shook her head, and pulled her hand away. 'Hardly. We only went out together half a dozen times.'

'Poor Jacob!'

Although he endeavoured to keep a mocking tone, Rafe couldn't help the feeling of relief that gripped him at this news. Yet once again he despised himself for the thought. He was almost forty, for God's sake, while she was—

Younger. Much younger.

Meanwhile, Lily had decided this conversation was getting far too personal. The dangers Dee-Dee had warned her about were patently obvious, and, to avoid any further familiarity, she clasped her hands tightly together in her lap.

'I must go,' she declared but, before she could gather her bag and get to her feet, Rafe spoke again.

'I thought you wanted to know why I came to visit with your father,' he said, and Lily's eyes widened in disbelief.

'I had heard that the good *padre* was interested in ancient texts,' Rafe put in swiftly. 'I have offered to lend him a script, reputed to have been written by William of Ockham. You have heard of him, *no*? He was a medieval scholar, to whom the argument that reason should have no part in faith was attributed.'

Lily hesitated. 'I wouldn't have thought such things would interest someone...someone...'

'Someone like me?' suggested Rafe mockingly. And when her face suffused again with becoming colour, he added, 'My uncle is a priest, *pequeña*. It is amazing how useful his knowledge of religion can be.'

CHAPTER SIX

THEY LEFT THE small restaurant soon after and, to Lily's relief, there was no sign of the photographer.

And it was quite pleasant walking casually along the quayside, chatting about inconsequential things. Lily was pleased to discover that Rafe enjoyed swimming too and that, like her father had said, he did have a sailing craft of his own.

It was as they walked past the park that Rafe said softly, 'Why do you not show me where you usually have lunch? It was here, was it not, instead of the restaurant, *no*?'

Lily was taken aback. 'I ought to be getting back to the agency,' she said, realising with a pang that Rafe had said nothing about his own possible involvement with the business. 'I...well... I've already had longer than I should.'

'Myers can manage without you for a few more minutes,' Rafe declared, his hand on the small of her back guiding her into the park. He stopped beside a vacant wooden bench. 'Shall we sit here?'

Lily hesitated. 'Why?'

'I enjoy your company,' he said simply. 'And I would like to enjoy it a little longer. Is that so hard to believe?'

It was, but Lily sat down anyway. And Rafe Oliveira sat down beside her, his arm along the back of the bench, only inches from the nape of her neck.

Rafe clenched his hand convulsively. The urge to touch the soft curve of skin so close to his fingers was almost irresistible. How would she react, he wondered, if he tangled his fingers in the silky strands of hair that had escaped from the knot she'd secured earlier? What would she do if he bent and placed his lips against her smooth skin? Would she run a mile?

Possibly.

He stifled an inward groan. For God's sake, what was he doing? She was probably—what?—fifteen years younger than he was, and he had no desire to add cradle-snatching to his other sins. He would certainly have her father breathing fire down his neck if he attempted to deepen their relationship.

So he said the first thing that came into his head. 'Tell me about Cartagena Charters. I think you probably know more about the company than Myers.'

Lily caught her breath at that and, when she turned her head to look at him, he wasn't surprised to see the accusation in her eyes.

'Is that why you really asked me to come into the park?' she exclaimed. 'Because you wanted to talk about the agency? Was the restaurant not private enough for you?'

'Do not be ridiculous.' Rafe found he was a little impatient now. 'You cannot possibly believe I would do such a thing.'

'But I don't know you, Señor Oliveira. I don't know what your motives are,' she declared staunchly. 'And you can't expect me to discuss Ray's business with you. He may be foolish at times, but we have worked together for too many years for me to let him down.'

She would have got to her feet then, but his hand on her knee was so shocking that she remained where she was. But that didn't prevent her stomach from tightening again, or ease the erratic tattoo of her heart.

Rafe regarded her, aware that once again he had said the wrong thing. She distrusted him now and was unlikely to believe anything he said.

Her knee jerked beneath his fingers and he removed his hand. 'Whatever you think, I am interested in the agency. And, in my opinion, you seem eminently aware of what is going on, *no*?'

Lily took a steadying breath. She knew that if she had any sense she'd get up and leave before he said anything else.

And before she was tempted to warn him that Ray couldn't always be trusted to tell the truth.

'I would prefer it if you addressed any queries you have about the agency to Ray, *señor*,' she said stiffly. 'Please don't think that buying me lunch will persuade me to betray any problems Ray might be having to you.'

Rafe's mouth took on a cynical twist. So Myers was having problems. She wasn't aware of it, but she'd as good as said so.

But he wasn't foolish enough to reveal her mistake. On the contrary, her impulsive words had only made him even more attracted to her than he already was.

Lily, however, had decided she'd said enough. Besides, she was far too conscious of the warm strength of his thigh next to hers. And although she tried to tell herself it was the sun, shining through the branches of the tree under which the bench was situated, that was causing her skin to take on a sheen of perspiration, the truth was she felt hot all over when he looked at her as he was doing now.

'I did not mean to upset you,' he said huskily, and an involuntary shiver ran down her spine. 'I forget you are so young. And innocent in the ways of the world.'

'Innocent?' Lily returned his gaze now. 'I'm not a child, *señor*.'

'Perhaps it is just that you seem so—unworldly to a man like me,' he ventured reluctantly, and she frowned.

'Why a man like you?'

'Oh.' He gave a wry smile. 'Because of my background, I suppose.'

'You mean because…because…'

'Because I have been in prison?' he queried. '*Sí*, that was not a good time in my life.'

Lily stared at him. 'Actually, I didn't know you'd been in prison,' she said, feeling awkward now. 'You said that you were...that you were...'

'Innocent?' he queried 'That is true. But it took my lawyers some time to prove it, *no*?'

He paused and then went on evenly, '*No obstante*, these things change you, change your personality. I am not the ignorant child I was when I left Cuba.'

'But you are Cuban?'

'Partly,' Rafe agreed. 'My father is Cuban but my mother was an Americano. After the Revolution, he and my mother lived there for several more years before they were able to make their escape.'

'They escaped?' Lily was fascinated in spite of herself. 'What an interesting history your family must have.' She forgot for a moment all about Ray and the agency. 'Mine is so boring by comparison. My parents left England when I was a baby. I don't really remember living anywhere else but here.'

Rafe's eyes darkened. 'Believe me, there is nothing boring about you, *querida*,' he assured her roughly, his voice thickening and scraping across her already sensitised nerves. His lips twisted. 'Do not be deceived. Many women would envy you your lack of—what shall I say?—artificiality, *no*?'

'Many women?' Lily bit her lip. 'And I suppose you've known lots.'

'Some,' Rafe agreed evenly, determined not to be

drawn into further intimacy. He forced a self-mocking smile. 'I am quite old, *al fin y al cabo*.'

Lily frowned. 'I don't think you're old.'

'But I am,' he told her with a careless shrug. 'Much older than you, *no*?'

Lily took an uneven breath. 'What you're really saying is that you're so much more experienced than me.'

Rafe rose to his feet at her words. This was getting much too personal. He suspected she was unaware of his reaction to her words, but the temptation she offered was getting under his skin. His height giving him an added advantage, he said tersely, 'I think you should leave, *niña*.' He used the childish term deliberately in an effort to control the madness that was lurking inside him. 'You may tell your father I will let him have the text he is interested in in the next few days.'

Lily hesitated but when he held out his hand she rose slowly from the bench. 'Do you want to get rid of me now, *señor*?' she asked, amazed that she was speaking so confidently when, in effect, her nerves were drawn as tight as violin strings.

'*Cara,*' he said tightly, 'I have enjoyed our conversation. But, as you said a few moments ago, Myers will be wondering where you are.'

Lily lifted her shoulders in a careless gesture and Rafe's eyes were instantly drawn to the revealing vee of her shirt. He glimpsed the swell of her breasts, the dusky hollow between. The lacy curve of a bra had never looked more inviting, and he knew he should step away.

She was so sweet but so vulnerable, he thought grimly. And, for his sins, he wanted her. Wanted a woman who, for all her foolish provocation, was still much too immature for him.

'You're right,' she said, lifting her eyes to his, and he wondered what she thought of his dismissal. 'And at least Ray respects my opinion.'

'What is that supposed to mean?' Rafe scowled. 'I cannot believe you care what that—*imbecil*—thinks of you.'

'Ray's not an imbecile,' she exclaimed defensively. 'I—I like him. We—we are good together.'

Rafe looked horror-stricken. 'You cannot mean that you have feelings for this man. Oh, Lily, I do not want to hurt you, but you have so much to learn about the world in general and men in particular.'

Lily's lips parted. 'If you're implying that I've never been with a man—' she began, and then pressed a hand to her mouth as if by doing so she could take back the childish words.

Holding up her head, she added, trying for inconsequence, 'In any case, it wasn't very illuminating, as I recall.'

'Then you slept with the wrong man,' said Rafe, his tone thickening, and he felt an unwelcome irritation at the thought.

He shifted impatiently, uncomfortably aware of his unwanted arousal. Then, as another thought occurred to him, 'Please tell me it was not Myers who gave you such a poor opinion of my sex.'

'I don't think that's anything to do with you,' Lily retorted shortly. Just who did he think he was? 'If you'll excuse me, *señor*—'

But Rafe had had enough. Against his better judgement, he caught her wrist when she would have turned away. His fingers registered warm skin, a racing pulse and the vulnerable spread of veins beneath his hand.

And his brain logged on to the knowledge that they were virtually alone in this corner of the park.

He wanted to kiss her, he thought grimly. He wanted to feel that soft mouth beneath his own. Ignoring his conscience, ignoring everything he'd told himself since they'd left the agency, he rubbed the smooth flesh that was virtually locked within his grasp against his lower body.

His arousal hardened immediately. And she couldn't fail to be aware of it. Just the touch of those slim fingers against his manhood had him catching his breath. Heat swept through his loins, leaving him taut and vulnerable. Whether he'd intended to kiss her or not, the question was now moot.

With a groan that was part protest, part relief, he gave in to the desire to taste her. Her mouth was soft and pliant, and unexpectedly hot. Still finding it difficult to breathe, he pulled her even closer, plundering her willing sweetness with his tongue until he was forced to take a breath.

Her submission had been as incredible as it was eager and when he dragged his mouth from hers he buried his face in the hollow between her shoulder and her neck.

'Por dios!' he muttered hoarsely, aware that he was near to losing it. But when she gave a little moan and wound her arms around his neck, Rafe knew he had fallen into a trap of his own making.

As he inhaled her scent, he knew he'd never dreamt that he might be seduced by her youth and inexperience. How could he have known that her lips might excite and inflame him until his body was bathed in her heat? When he'd thrust his tongue into her mouth, he'd revelled in its possession. *Dios mio*, his control had almost been swept away.

Aware that the fire he had created was threatening to consume him, Rafe's hands curled about her nape. Her silky hair tumbled about his fingers, and he badly wanted to go on kissing her. But this was madness, he told himself. It couldn't be allowed to win.

'Mierda,' he muttered, dragging his mouth across the smooth curve of her cheek. 'This should not be happening.'

He forced himself to step back from her, avoiding the confused glance she cast in his direction. 'Take my advice: stay away from me in future,' he added harshly. 'I may not be so—so generous next time.'

CHAPTER SEVEN

Lily was having supper with her father a couple of evenings later when she heard the unmistakable sound of a car pulling up outside the rectory.

Immediately, her mouth dried and her heart increased its pace until it was banging crazily against her ribcage. They weren't expecting any visitors, and the only person she could think of who might call after dark was Rafe Oliveira.

It might be Ray Myers, of course. He was a friend of her father's and occasionally called in for a chat. But, in the present circumstances, she didn't think that was likely as he'd barely spoken to her since Rafe Oliveira had walked out of the agency.

Thankfully, Ray knew nothing about her having lunch with the man, or—her skin prickled—what had come after. When she'd returned to the agency, he'd immediately blamed her for not supporting him and warned her that if things didn't improve she might be out of a job.

And Lily had known he wasn't joking.

So if it was Oliveira she would have to be polite. But what was he doing here? Could he possibly have come to apologise? No, he'd probably brought the text he'd promised to lend her father, she assured herself. Whatever had happened between them, she had the feeling that Oliveira was a man who always kept his word.

When the expected knock came at the door, her father wiped his mouth on his napkin. Then he picked up the plate of gumbo that Dee-Dee had left for their evening meal and got up from the table.

'Get that, will you, Lily?' he asked rather irritably. He never liked being interrupted during a meal. 'Unless it's an emergency, I'm working. I'll finish this in my study.'

Lily's heart was beating fast again as she went to answer the door. Earlier, at her father's insistence, she'd shed the shorts and shirt she'd worn to work in favour of an ankle-length chemise dress. Now, she was glad of its length to hide her shaky knees.

But when she opened the door she looked with some surprise at her visitor. 'Laura!' she exclaimed blankly. It was months, possibly even years, since she and Laura Mathews had spoken to one another. 'What are you doing here?'

It wasn't the most enthusiastic of greetings and Laura pulled a rueful face. 'Hi,' she said casually. 'I know it's been a while, but I was passing and I just thought I'd call and see how you were getting on.'

Lily was still trying to decide what to say when Laura spoke again. 'May I come in?'

'I—oh, of course.' Lily moved aside automatically and Laura stepped into the hall. 'Go into the living room. I'll make some coffee.'

'That would be nice.' But, instead of doing as Lily had asked, Laura followed her down the hall and into the kitchen with an unwelcome familiarity. 'This place doesn't change much, does it?'

'Do you mean this house or the island?' Lily asked, tamping down her resentment at Laura's words.

'Well, everything, actually,' replied Laura carelessly. 'I did wonder if you'd be married by now.'

Lily was fairly sure she hadn't wondered any such thing, but she took the girl's words at face value. 'Not me,' she said as the coffee started filtering into the jug. Her lips twisted. 'How about you?'

Laura lounged into one of the chairs at the scrubbed pine table and gave a shrug. 'I've had offers,' she declared. 'But I guess I'm too picky.' She propped her arms on the table. 'So, how are you? How is your father?'

'We're fine.' Lily managed a smile. 'Working hard, as usual. Daddy and I don't see a lot of one another, actually. He's always in his study.'

'Still composing those fire and brimstone sermons, hmm?' murmured Laura mockingly. 'I wonder if he really scares his congregation.'

'I don't think his sermons are meant to scare anyone,' said Lily evenly. 'And I don't recall them threatening fire and brimstone either.'

'Oh, you know what I mean.' Laura waved a flippant hand in front of her face. 'You have to admit, he does take himself rather seriously, Lily. Grant says all Presbyterians are like that.'

'I doubt Grant Mathews has been inside a church often enough to make such a judgement,' returned Lily tartly.

She didn't like Laura making fun of her father, or the girl's habit of calling her own father by his first name. It seemed disrespectful somehow, but she was probably old-fashioned.

'Hey, I was only joking.' Laura watched Lily taking mugs down from the wall cupboard with reproachful eyes. 'So—are you still working at the agency?'

'Yes, that's right,' agreed Lily. 'What about you? Have you given up your job in New York?'

'Sort of. I was bored of it.'

Laura spoke carelessly enough, but Lily had a sudden presentiment that the other girl wasn't telling the whole truth. Laura simply didn't want to admit the truth of why she had come back.

'Are you staying long?' asked Lily, wondering again why the girl was here. They seemed to have little in common these days.

'I'm not sure.' Laura shrugged. 'But that's enough about me.' She regarded Lily with strangely speculative eyes. 'Tell me what's been happening on the island. Have you met any exciting men lately?'

Lily was glad to see that the coffee was ready. With colour rising up her throat, she went to fill the mugs. 'Do you have to ask?'

'I think so.' Laura's expertly shaped brows drew together. 'From what I've heard, you haven't been spending all your time working at the agency or looking after Daddy.'

There was sarcasm and a certain bitterness in her words and Lily glanced over her shoulder with startled eyes. 'What have you heard?'

'I understand you've been seen with our oh-so-notorious new resident,' Laura remarked, her eyes narrowed in accusation. 'Don't tell me you don't know who I mean.'

Lily lifted the jug, hoping she could pour the coffee without spilling it. 'Do you mean Mr Oliveira?' she asked casually, filling the mugs with a determined hand. She lifted one and set it down in front of Laura. 'There you go. Do you want cream or sugar?'

'Neither.' Laura made a careless gesture and took a sip.

Then, realising something more was needed, 'Thanks.'

'My pleasure.'

Although it wasn't really. However, guessing Laura intended to stay in the kitchen, Lily excused herself from her visitor and carried one of the mugs through to the study.

'It's Laura Mathews,' she told her father flatly. And, at his look of enquiry, 'Yes, I was surprised too.'

Back in the kitchen, Laura had left the table and was pouring herself another mug of the black brew. 'You don't mind, do you?' she asked, raising the pot as Lily came in. 'I need this.'

Lily shrugged. 'Help yourself,' she said, taking a carton of milk from the fridge and adding a little to her own coffee. Then she joined the other girl at the table. 'What's this all about?'

'What's what all about?' Laura asked, feigning ignorance.

'Your being here,' said Lily drily. 'We're not usually on your visiting list.'

Laura blew out a breath. Then, after a few moments' consideration, she got to the point.

'Tell me about "Mr Oliveira",' she said, making imaginary quotes around his name. 'I understand you know him quite well.'

'Hardly.' Lily was determined not to be drawn. 'I believe he has an interest in the agency. That's all.'

'Really?' Laura put down her mug and regarded Lily with some scepticism. 'So what were you doing having lunch with him a couple of days ago?'

Lily flushed. She couldn't help it. She should have known that a juicy piece of gossip like that wouldn't escape the island grapevine. She swallowed. She only hoped that no one knew what had happened after the meal.

Now, realising there was no point denying it, she said, 'I did have lunch with him, yes. I...well, he saved me from being killed by a speeding minibus, and he insisted on taking me somewhere where I could sit down and recover.'

'How cosy.' Laura didn't sound as if she believed her. 'I didn't know Oliveira was such a considerate man.'

'Didn't you?' Once again, Lily sensed the undercurrent in her words. Then, tentatively, 'But I thought your father was a friend of his.'

Laura snorted. 'What gave you that impression?'

Lily frowned. 'I suppose because he now owns the house at Orchid Point.'

Laura sniffed impatiently. 'I see you've heard about Grant's misfortune in Las Vegas.' She scowled. 'I suppose that horrid little woman told you.'

Lily's lips parted. 'What horrid little woman?'

'You know. She works for you—or she used to. Nothing happens on Orchid Cay without the voodoo priestess knowing all about it.'

'If you mean Dee-Dee—'

'Of course I mean Dee-Dee, if that's her name.' Laura was contemptuous. 'She never liked me, and people like her always envy people like Grant who succeed in life—'

Lily was tempted to say it was because Laura's father hadn't succeeded in life that the islanders were gossiping about him, but she held her tongue.

'Anyway,' Laura continued, 'Grant didn't sell the

house to Oliveira. He bought it from the man who won it from Grant in a rather dodgy game of poker.'

'I see.'

'So,' Laura went on insistently, 'tell me about Oliveira. What did you talk about? Have you been to the house?'

'Don't be ridiculous!' Lily was getting impatient now. 'I've told you, I hardly know the man. It's the agency he's interested in. Not me.'

'Well, if Ray Myers has any sense he'll steer well clear of him,' said Laura quickly. 'And you too, Lily. He's way out of your league.'

But not yours, thought Lily shrewdly, wondering if that was Laura's ulterior motive for being here. To warn Lily off.

'Well, thank you for that,' she said evenly. 'But I am old enough to make my own decisions, you know.'

'Not with men like him, you're not,' retorted Laura. 'I bet you don't know he has a conviction for drug smuggling. That's why he had to leave New York in such a hurry.'

'He doesn't—'

Lily started to say that Rafe hadn't been convicted of anything, but that would just be playing into the other girl's hands.

'And that's why his wife walked out on him too,' Laura continued knowingly. 'Although I have heard they've been seeing one another recently. Perhaps she's forgiven him. Who knows?' She took another sip of her coffee. 'I'm sorry if I've upset you, Lily, but you really need to know who you're associating with. If your father didn't always have his head stuck in some ancient text or other, he might see what's going on.'

'Daddy doesn't always have his head stuck in ancient texts,' Lily defended her father fiercely. She was beginning to wish that Laura would just go.

'Whatever.' Laura was indifferent. 'I just thought I ought to warn you, that's all. That man is not to be trusted.'

Rafe considered leaving the text he was loaning Lily's father at the agency. It would enable him to see Lily again without appearing as if he was looking to deepen their relationship. He had no desire to create a situation that might become difficult if he decided to invest in the business.

Or that was his excuse anyway.

Besides, he wanted to see Myers again. He'd had the man email the agency's profit and loss statements to him and he needed clarification on certain points concerning the figures.

But, somehow, the idea of turning up there on such a pretext might appear manufactured. Whatever way he looked at it, it would be easier to deliver the text to the Reverend Fielding himself.

He chose a time when he felt sure Lily would be at work.

He glanced at his watch as he parked outside the rectory and saw that it was barely eleven o'clock.

Hours before the agency closed its doors for lunch, even if it did so. Hours before Lily could be expected back at the rectory.

But when he walked towards the house, he glimpsed Lily working in the back garden. She'd evidently been deadheading some of the flowers, loading the vegetation into a small wheelbarrow, possibly to be used as compost later on.

In a sleeveless white vest and cotton shorts that exposed the slender length of her legs, she looked stunning. The vest revealed that she wasn't wearing a bra, and the shorts were evidently old and barely covered her bottom.

Dios, what was he thinking? Rafe was tempted to just turn around and go back to his car. But something, some extrasensory perception perhaps, caused her to look up and see him.

And then it was much too late to have second thoughts.

CHAPTER EIGHT

RAFE DIDN'T HAVE to be psychic to see Lily was startled. Her face suffused with brilliant colour, and he could almost see her pulling at the hem of her shorts.

Don't do that, he wanted to say, even though she represented everything he was trying to avoid. But there was no denying his reaction to her, however inappropriate that reaction might be.

'What are you doing here?' she exclaimed at once, abandoning the wheelbarrow and facing him across the width of the garden.

And Rafe couldn't blame her for the question. After all, he had said she should avoid him in future.

'I brought the text for your father,' he said, making no attempt to approach her. 'I assumed you would be at work.'

'Oh!' Was that disappointment he heard in her voice, or was that only wishful thinking? 'Well, Daddy's not here. From time to time, he conducts services on the adjoining island, San Columba. He left this morning. He'll be back later today.'

'I see.' Rafe fingered the wrapping on the book he'd brought for her father to see. 'That is a pity. It seems I must leave this theological text with you.'

'Or you could come back tomorrow,' Lily suggested stiffly. 'I'm sure Daddy would like to thank you personally for your interest.'

So polite!

Rafe expelled an impatient breath. Was he really responsible for her present attitude? He feared so. And why, when he knew he should be grateful, was he so reluctant to turn around and go away?

The rustle of clothing behind him had him glancing swiftly over his shoulder—only to find an elderly West Indian woman, wearing a long multi-coloured dress, regarding him from the porch.

Dee-Dee, he assumed, remembering what Carla had told him. Tall and obviously overweight, she had the sharpest brown eyes he had ever seen, and they were presently regarding him with a mixture of wariness and suspicion.

'You need any help, girl?' she asked, her eyes switching to Lily, and Rafe could almost feel the girl's relief at their stilted tête-à-tête being interrupted.

'No.' Lily took off the clumsy gardening gloves which she'd been using to deadhead the plants and dropped them on the low stone wall that edged the flower beds. 'Um… Mr Oliveira was just leaving.' She paused. 'He's brought a book for Daddy to see so perhaps you could take it, Dee-Dee? My hands are dirty.'

'No problem.'

Dee-Dee came down off the porch and Rafe was obliged to put his parcel into her hands. Hands that were adorned with an assortment of rings, he noticed, henna-painted symbols on her fingers adding to the tattoos that covered her ample arms.

'How you liking living on our island, Mr Oliveira?' she asked as she tucked the package under her arm, and Rafe felt obliged to answer her.

'Very much,' he said, his gaze flicking almost compulsively in Lily's direction. 'It is certainly a change from what I am used to.'

'Y—e—s.' The woman drew out the word, regarding him through narrowed lids. 'Orchid Cay is nothing like New York. I'll give you that.'

'No.' Rafe wished she'd go back into the house so that he could at least say goodbye to Lily in private. 'Much warmer, I think.'

'I suppose that depends if we're talking about the climate,' remarked Dee-Dee, her lips twisting mockingly, and to his relief Lily decided to intervene.

'I don't think the reason why Mr Oliveira chose to leave New York is any of our business, Dee-Dee,' she said, but for the first time that day a trace of amusement lurked at the corner of her mouth. 'Put the parcel in Daddy's study, will you? That way he'll see it as soon as he gets home.'

'If you say so.' Dee-Dee was evidently not liking being dismissed so summarily. 'You need me, you just yell, right?'

'I will.'

The two women exchanged a speaking look and, without any other alternative, Dee-Dee turned and went back to the house.

'Your housekeeper does not trust me,' Rafe remarked as the West Indian woman disappeared indoors, and Lily sighed.

'Dee-Dee is protective of me, that's all.' She bit her lower lip and once again Rafe was disturbed by the urge he had to taste the luscious fullness of her mouth. 'And now you'll have to excuse me too. I've been working in the garden since Daddy left and I need a shower.'

Rafe inclined his head, once again tormented by images of her naked, the water cascading off tip-tilted breasts and deliciously rounded hips.

Trying to ground himself, he muttered, 'Is there some reason why you are not working at the agency?' He paused and then went on harshly, 'Do not tell me Myers has dismissed you for having lunch with me.'

'For being late back, perhaps?' Lily shook her head. 'No. But when Daddy is away, someone needs to be here at the rectory in case they're needed.' She paused. 'Besides, I've been working late a couple of nights this week and I was due the time off.'

Rafe nodded, wondering what she'd been working on. A second set of financial statements, perhaps? Sooner or later, he'd have to speak to Myers himself.

'So,' she murmured, taking a step in his direction, 'if that's all…' She paused. 'I have to visit one of Daddy's parishioners this afternoon.'

Rafe wanted to say more; in truth he wanted to ask her to spend the rest of the day with him, but common sense prevailed.

'Please tell your father I was sorry to miss him,' he said politely.

'*Adios*, Ms Fielding. It was very nice seeing you again.'

Lily sat at her desk in the inner office of the agency, listening to Ray trying to defend his decision to hire the *Santa Lucia* out to customers when its engines had been badly in need of an overhaul.

The group from Boston who'd hired the *Lucia* for a fishing trip had been forced to make landfall in Montego Bay when one of the engines had failed. The group had had to limp into the port and fly back to Orchid Cay from Jamaica.

At present, the two men who had organised the trip were in the agency, demanding not just their money back but the price of their air tickets as well. And Lily couldn't blame them.

In her opinion, Ray was lucky not to be facing calls for compensation or criminal charges, or both. If a storm had blown up while the *Lucia* was disabled, he might well be having to defend his actions to the port authorities instead of two irate bankers.

She sighed. Ray was a fool. He always played the odds and usually the odds were against him. Like this business with Rafe Oliveira, for instance. Did he honestly think he could get away with falsifying the figures he'd emailed to the other man? Lily was sure it would take someone infinitely more cunning than Ray Myers to get one over on him.

There was the sound of a hand slamming down on the counter and a few hushed threatening words and then—silence. Had the men gone or were they still there, waiting for some response from Ray?

She had her answer a few moments later when Ray himself ambled round the screen and regarded her dourly. 'Bloody morons,' he said angrily. 'Who the hell do they think they are?'

Lily breathed a little more freely. 'What happened?'

Ray gave her a scornful look. 'As if you didn't hear. They're coming back tomorrow for their money. If I don't have it, they're going to report me to the authorities. I could lose my licence. What the hell am I going to do?'

Lily licked her lips. 'You shouldn't have let them take the *Lucia*,' she said carefully, and Ray swore.

'Tell me something I don't know,' he snarled, kicking at the corner of the filing cabinet as he passed. 'I needed that charter. You know I did. I've told you how tight things are at present. What was I supposed to do? Turn down a potential fortune in future sales?'

'Well, that's not going to happen now, is it?'

'You have a knack for stating the bloody obvious, you know that?' Ray swore again. 'If you can't think of something constructive to say, keep your mouth shut. The last thing I need is someone saying *I told you so!*'

'I'm sorry.' Lily slid off her chair. 'Well, now seems as good a time as any to go for my lunch. It's after one o'clock already. And as I'm not being of any help—'

Ray's jaw clenched but then he gave her a remorseful look. 'Take no notice of me,' he muttered, by way of an apology. 'I know you mean well, but right now I need solutions not advice.'

Lily bent and picked up her bag and hooked it over her shoulder. 'Why don't you take a break too? I'm going to get a sandwich. You should do the same. You might feel more optimistic after you've filled your lungs with fresh air.'

'I wouldn't count on it,' said Ray dourly, but he pulled his hands out of his pants pockets and considered her suggestion. 'I guess I could do with a beer,' he added, nodding. 'How about joining me for a drink?'

Lily sighed. She really didn't want to escape from the charged atmosphere of the agency into the smoky atmosphere of a bar.

But Ray looked so mournful, she couldn't say no. 'Okay,' she said. 'But just one drink. Then I'm going to get myself something to eat.'

'They serve food at Mac's Bar.'

'Yes, but I'd prefer to eat outdoors.' Lily hoped that would end the discussion. 'Shall we go?'

To her relief, Ray's misgivings about closing the agency for an hour diverted him from pursuing the eating debate any further. He was still chuntering on about how they might be missing an important booking when they reached the bar on Front Street.

A striped awning shadowed a porch that gave onto the dark interior, an impression that was heightened by stepping out of the noonday sun.

'As we haven't had a customer all morning, I don't think that's likely,' Lily was saying as she preceded him inside. 'Relax, Ray. Let's try and think of some way to solve your money problems.'

The bar was fairly crowded despite the summer heat, and Mac, the elderly Scotsman who'd opened the place almost thirty years ago, had pushed wide the louvres to allow the heat and smoke to escape.

Most people stood around the bar, and the hum of conversation was predictably noisy. Mac didn't discriminate, and his clientele mixed fishermen with millionaires.

There were a handful of tables set out on a deck at the back of the building, but these tables were usually taken. Lily resigned herself to standing while she sipped her glass of iced tea.

'Is there no chance of getting a table?' Ray asked, returning with what looked like a vodka and tonic instead of the beer she'd expected. 'Have you checked the deck?'

'Well—no.' But Lily wasn't optimistic.

'Let's see then, shall we?'

Ray pushed his way through the throng congregated around the bar, and Lily was forced to follow or lose sight of him altogether.

An open archway led outdoors and stepping out into the brilliant sunshine was almost as blinding as entering the dark bar had been earlier. For a few moments, Lily stood there blinking in the sudden brightness while Ray scanned the canopied deck with a practised eye.

And then, as her vision cleared, Lily saw someone she recognised immediately. Rafe Oliveira was sitting at a table at the far side of the wooden structure. In a black tee shirt and khaki cargo pants, he stood out among the colourful island shirts and baggy trousers.

As if sensing her startled regard, he lifted his head at that moment and their eyes met. For a few loaded seconds Lily couldn't look away.

But then Ray spoke and she came to her senses, turning to him like a life raft in a stormy sea. 'Sorry, what did you say?'

'I said it looks fairly crowded,' muttered Ray gloomily, taking a generous mouthful of his drink. 'Wouldn't you know it? I never have any luck.'

'Why don't we go somewhere else then?' suggested Lily hastily. She was desperate to get out of the bar now. God, she so didn't want to have to deal with Oliveira again.

'But where?'

Ray was still looking about him with a brooding gaze when a hand descended on Lily's shoulder. Long fingers gripped the fine bones beneath her thin cotton sweater, causing the loose neckline to slip dangerously down her arm.

'This is a surprise,' Rafe said, controlling the unwarranted fury he felt at seeing her with the other man. 'I did not expect to find you in a bar.'

His voice was low but disturbingly sensual, and Lily saw Ray's eyes widen at the implied intimacy of Oliveira's words.

But he had other things on his mind.

'Hey, Mr Oliveira,' he said enthusiastically. 'What are you doing here? Were you looking for me?'

Rafe's lips twisted. Why in God's name would the fool think that? 'I regret, no,' he said with studied politeness. His hand dropped reluctantly from Lily's shoulder as she shifted out of his reach. 'Are you staying for lunch?'

'No.' Lily took the initiative. 'When Ray's finished his drink, we're leaving.'

'Are we?' Ray could be annoyingly obtuse. Didn't he realise he was the last person Oliveira would go looking for? He looked at the other man. 'As a matter of fact, we were hoping to find a vacant table, but it looks as if we're out of luck.'

Rafe scowled. He didn't like being put on the spot by anybody and particularly not when the situation was of his own making. If he hadn't left his seat, he wouldn't be in this position.

He knew what Myers was up to, of course. The other man saw this as the ideal opportunity to do a little friendly networking. But what Myers didn't know was that Rafe would prefer not to introduce his companion to Lily.

It was crazy, he knew, but he didn't want her to think he was at all interested in Laura Mathews. He wondered now why, in heaven's name, he had even agreed to meet her.

However, avoiding the issue with Laura would only hint at a hidden agenda. Speaking stiffly, he said, 'Perhaps you would like to join me? I am with a guest, but I am sure she will not mind.'

Lily badly wanted to refuse the invitation. She'd been reluctant to stay before, but now, hearing Oliveira say he had a female guest made the situation even more unbearable.

Who could it be? she wondered tensely, and unwillingly Laura's warning came into her mind. His ex-wife, perhaps? Had she followed him to the island? Dear God, why had she thought that having a drink with Ray would be simple? Now she was going to be forced to be civil to a woman Oliveira was probably sleeping with.

Oh, dear Lord.

'That's awfully good of you.' While she'd been staring into her glass, trying to find a solution in the rapidly melting ice cubes, Ray had been congratulating himself for squeezing an invitation out of the other man. 'As it happens, I was hoping to have a brief word about the balance sheets I sent you. They don't tell the whole story, you know, and I'd welcome the opportunity to discuss them with you.'

'I never mix business with pleasure,' said Rafe tightly, and then wished he'd used other words. His lunchtime drink with Grant Mathews's daughter could hardly be described as pleasure. 'My table is over here.'

Ray noticed the expression on Lily's face as she was forced to follow the two men across the deck. He arched his eyebrows at her. 'What? What?' he asked with an innocent air, but Lily wasn't deceived.

'Five minutes; that's all I'm staying,' she hissed. 'If I'd known what you had in mind, I'd never have come into the bar.'

'Hey, I didn't know he was here,' muttered Ray defensively. 'And what's your problem? You two seemed pretty friendly earlier on. And how did he know you don't normally drink at lunchtime? If I didn't know better, I'd say he was making a pass.'

Lily gasped. 'Don't be so ridiculous!' she exclaimed, hoping he would attribute her heightened colour to the effects of the sun. Remembering what had happened in Palmetto Park, those words were definitely not appropriate.

Rafe glanced over his shoulder at that moment and once again she met his brooding gaze. He didn't look pleased, she conceded. It seemed obvious he was as unwilling to have them join his party as she was.

Ray suddenly nudged her arm, almost causing her to spill what was left of her drink. 'Look at that,' he muttered. 'See who his guest is. It's Laura Mathews, as I live and breathe. My God, it hasn't taken her long to reel him in!'

CHAPTER NINE

LAURA!

Lily came to an abrupt halt. Laura Mathews was Oliveira's guest! Not his wife; not some other woman he'd brought to Orchid Cay; not even someone Lily didn't know that he'd met while he was here. But Laura Mathews. As Ray had said, she hadn't wasted any time.

Lily couldn't take it in. After the way the other girl had warned her about Oliveira, warned her to stay away from him indeed, it was unbelievable. Yet there Laura sat, elegant in a slinky satin halter top and low-rise Capri pants, sipping a cocktail as if she hadn't a care in the world.

'Come on.' Ray was getting impatient and he reached back and grabbed Lily's arm, yanking her forward. 'You know Laura, don't you? I seem to remember the two of you used to be friends.'

Used to be being the operative phrase, thought Lily bitterly, remembering Laura's visit to the rectory with some annoyance. It was obvious now that Laura had had an agenda of her own.

Rafe paused by the stripped pine table where his guest was sitting, and Laura turned her head to give him a warm smile. She probably wouldn't be smiling when she discovered he'd invited the others to join them, he mused, reaching for his glass and taking a long welcome gulp of cold beer.

Aware that Lily was behind him, he said tersely, 'I've invited a couple of acquaintances to join us, Laura. I am sure you will not object.'

'Acquaintances?' Laura said, with a frown drawing her arched brows together. It was clear his announcement hadn't pleased her. 'Who?' she asked, half irritably, almost as if she had the right to decide who joined them.

'You will see,' Rafe declared, stepping aside, and saw the way Laura's face contorted when she saw the other girl.

'Lily Fielding,' she muttered in an undertone, but Rafe heard her.

'You know her?'

Laura forced a smile for the other girl's benefit. 'Of course we know one another. It's good to see you again, Lily.'

'Is it?'

Lily was hardly enthusiastic, and Rafe was aware of an undercurrent that he couldn't quite figure out.

'Why do we not sit down,' he suggested pleasantly, as a waiter arrived to take their order. He looked at the remains of Lily's drink. 'Can I get you another one of those?'

'No, thanks.' Much against her better judgement, Lily slipped into the seat beside Laura. 'I won't be staying long.'

Rafe's lips tightened, but he made no response. While he ordered another piña colada for Laura, a vodka and tonic for Ray, and a beer for himself, Lily regarded the other girl through narrowed eyes.

'Fancy seeing you here, Laura,' she said. 'I thought at first Mr Oliveira's companion must be his wife, particularly as you gave me the impression that you didn't know him.'

'You must be mistaken,' returned Laura coldly and, when her drink arrived, she hid her face behind the glass.

'Obviously.' Lily took a mouthful of her drink, which was now not much more than melting ice cubes. 'I'm sorry if Ray and I have interrupted something.'

She met Oliveira's eyes challengingly across the rim of her glass, and his lips tightened in response. 'Ms Mathews's father used to own Orchid Point,' he said flatly, but he was sure she knew this already. 'She was telling me the history of the house.'

'Really?' Lily was amazed how relaxed she sounded when inside her stomach was roiling. 'Has your father sent you out on a charm offensive, Laura?'

Rafe reflected that it was just as well he wasn't holding a wine glass at that moment. It might well have shattered in his hand. He'd never have expected

Lily would have the nerve to take his luncheon companion on, but she was gazing at the other girl with undisguised dislike.

Deciding he needed to calm the situation, Rafe spoke. His free hand balling into a fist, he said, 'I agreed to meet Laura for a drink because she has come to the house a couple of times and I have been unavailable,' he stated harshly. 'And, just for the record, *Ms* Fielding, I do not have a wife.'

Lily shrugged. 'I'm sorry,' she said, though he sensed she wasn't. 'Is Mr Mathews a friend of yours?'

Hardly, thought Rafe dourly but, before he could speak, Myers chose to intervene. 'Come on, Lily,' he said. 'That's privileged information.' He paused and then added, 'Although I had heard your father was having some financial difficulties, Laura.'

Laura was obviously seething, Lily could tell. And, while she had no reason to feel sorry for the girl, she couldn't let Ray get away with that. 'We all have money problems from time to time,' she said warningly. 'You know that.'

Laura snorted. 'I don't need you to defend me, Lily,' she exclaimed. 'And while it is true I was hoping to pick Rafe's brains about Daddy's possible investments, that's not the only reason I'm here.'

Lily could believe that, and she resorted once again to her glass. But, to her annoyance, she saw that it was empty, and she contented herself with running her fingertips around the rim.

The others didn't have that problem, and Ray lost

no time in finishing his first drink and starting on his second. Lily knew it was only a matter of time before he brought up the agency's balance sheets again, and she wanted no part of any lies he might be planning to tell Oliveira.

'Look,' she said, before the conversation could become more general, 'I think I ought to go. I've got some shopping to do before I go back to work and Ray doesn't like leaving the agency closed for too long, do you, Ray?'

Ray's jaw compressed but, short of asking her to stay and back him up, his hands were tied. 'If that's what you want to do, I can't stop you,' he muttered sulkily. 'But, like you told me earlier, it is lunchtime. We all deserve a break.'

Me more than most, thought Lily grimly, not at all swayed by Ray's unsubtle plea. She got to her feet, avoiding Oliveira's eyes as he got up also. 'Goodbye, Laura. Goodbye, Mr Oliveira.' She glanced in her employer's direction. 'I expect I'll see you later, Ray.'

Always providing he could stagger back to the agency after having goodness knew how many vodka and tonics on an empty stomach, she reflected as she strode quickly across the deck and pushed her way through the bar crowd to the exit.

But she was grateful to be out of there. She knew that if she'd stayed any longer, she might have said something she'd regret.

She was aware of someone behind her as she stepped out of the bar into the sunlight. Believing it to be another patron, she didn't hesitate before striding away along the street.

It was only when she paused at the edge of the pavement before crossing the road that she realised it was Oliveira. It was he who had been keeping pace with her, his hands shoved carelessly into the front pockets of his khaki pants.

'Hello again,' he said, meeting her startled gaze with cool enquiry. 'Do you mind telling me what that was all about?'

Lily expelled a nervous breath. 'I don't know what you mean.'

'I think you do.'

Rafe glanced up and down the street and then gripped her upper arm to escort her across the road. She shook him off almost at once, but that didn't stop her skin from tingling where he'd touched her.

And Rafe wasn't finished. 'What has Laura told you about me?' he demanded. 'And, equally significant, what has she told you about her father?'

'Laura wouldn't discuss her father with me,' she replied indifferently. She started to walk towards the sandwich kiosk, forcing him to walk with her. 'We move in different circles.'

Rafe shook his head. 'From what I gathered in there, you two do not like one another very much. Is her father involved?'

Lily gave him a swift look. 'I hardly know Grant Mathews.'

Rafe scowled. 'You know his daughter. And why she should need to tell lies about me, I do not understand.'

'Oh, please!' Lily had reached the kiosk and now she turned to face him with hostility in her eyes. 'Don't pretend you don't know what she was doing. Laura likes to stake her claim. You've just been given the winning ticket!'

She'd spoken coldly, the dislike in her tone evident, and Rafe's face darkened in anger. 'You are mistaken.'

'Am I? Oh, yes, I seem to be making a lot of mistakes today.' Lily snorted. 'I think it's time you were getting back to your guest, Mr Oliveira. You've neglected her long enough.'

No seas una idiota!' Rafe snapped, resisting the urge to take her by the shoulders and shake her. 'Do not be an idiot, Lily. Laura Mathews means nothing to me.'

'Perhaps you should tell her that.'

Rafe's jaw clamped on an expletive, but when he spoke again he had himself more in control. 'Do you think I care what she thinks? The woman has been trying to speak to me for the past week or more. Today—well, today, I chose to humour her.' He didn't give her his reasons. 'She was just getting round to telling me what she wanted when I saw you with Myers.'

'I'm sorry we disturbed you.' Lily didn't sound sympathetic and Rafe swore.

'Oh, you disturbed me, Lily. But not in the way you seem to think. How do you think I felt, seeing you with that *estupido*? The man is a fool. You can do better than him.'

Lily gasped. 'Who I choose to go out with isn't your concern, Mr Oliveira. And why should you care anyway? As I'm just another…acquaintance.'

Rafe's mouth compressed. 'You heard that?'

'Obviously.'

He scowled. 'So what would you have had me say? That we were more than friends?'

'We're not even friends, Mr Oliveira.' Lily bent her head and fumbled in her bag for her purse. 'And now, if you'll excuse me, I'm going to buy a sandwich for my lunch.'

Rafe expelled a weary breath. 'Lily, please. Do not treat me like a stranger. I realise I must have offended you, so let me make amends by buying you lunch.'

'Again?'

'Why not?'

'No, thanks.'

Lily tried to shake him off, but this time he wouldn't let her go. And, looking up into his dark impassioned face, she badly wanted to give in. 'What about your guest?' she protested, while her insides melted beneath his disturbing gaze. 'You are neglecting her.'

'Let Myers deal with her,' retorted Rafe harshly, detecting her indecision. 'Come! I know exactly the place for us to eat.'

* * *

Lily felt some trepidation when Rafe led the way to where he had parked his car. She had no idea he intended to drive to their destination.

'I can't be away long,' she protested when he opened the passenger door and indicated that she should get inside. 'Where are we going?'

'Not far,' said Rafe smoothly, coiling his length behind the wheel of the Lexus. 'There is a café at a place called Coral Key that the locals and the divers use. I believe the food—seafood, of course—is very good.'

Lily was still doubtful, but Rafe had apparently taken her silence for acceptance. The Lexus's powerful engine surged to life, and he drove smoothly out of the car parking area. He turned in the opposite direction from town, accelerating out onto the cliff road.

It wasn't until they turned onto a track that bypassed the little fishing village of Coral Key that Lily's reservations resurfaced.

'This is the way to Orchid Point,' she protested, giving him a horrified glance. 'I'm not going to your house.'

'Why not?'

'Because…because it's not appropriate.' She paused. 'Whatever you think of my father, he would definitely not approve.'

'But did you not tell me you were capable of making your own decisions?'

'I am.' Lily realised he had her there. 'But this isn't my decision. I'd like you to take me back to town at once.'

Rafe sighed. 'I just thought you might like to see what I have done with the house. And we can have a sandwich here without fear of interruption.'

They had reached the property now and the gates swung open at the press of a switch. The drive curved upward towards a white-painted villa with a pillared porch and a wraparound veranda, and Lily couldn't help admiring its sprawling elegance.

There were flowers everywhere, she noticed, growing over the frames of the many garages, tumbling in exotic confusion from the balconies above the porch. Giant urns spilled their bounty onto the steps that led up to the entrance, storm shutters painted a dark green contrasting with the whiteness of the walls.

'So,' he said, bringing the SUV to a halt, 'can I tempt you?'

Lily caught her breath, reluctantly getting out of the car. Did he know he tempted her already, his offer of lunch notwithstanding? Of course he did. Which was probably why he'd used that particular phrase.

'To have lunch with you?' she queried, and he gave a cynical nod as he alighted and walked round the car to meet her. 'So, I hear you own the house,' she said, needing to keep him at arm's length and, with a weary sigh, he inclined his head again.

'And you live here alone?'

'Hardly alone,' he replied drily. 'I need staff to keep this place going. Come and meet my house-keeper, Carla Samuels. Perhaps she will assure you, you are perfectly safe with me?'

CHAPTER TEN

THEY ENTERED THE house through a glass-walled entry that gave onto a sunlit reception area. It was a huge space with an attractively tiled floor, and more flowers decorating a large circular table in the centre.

Lily's eyes were immediately drawn to the stone staircase that wound to the upper gallery. She couldn't help wondering which of the many rooms opening onto the landing was Rafe's.

Across the hall a beautiful sitting room had a panoramic view of the bay. Once again, the room was generously proportioned, with several comfortable sofas and chairs in a warm bronze leather. The terrazzo tiled floor was scattered with Chinese rugs, and there were dark cabinets, filled with books and objets d'art, against the walls.

'Carla will get us something to eat,' said Rafe as Lily moved to where glass doors gave onto a shaded patio, and she glanced back in some alarm.

'Oh, but—'

'You do not want to be long,' Rafe finished for her flatly. 'I know. Just give me a minute, will you?'

He disappeared into the entrance hall again and Lily put her hand on the cool glass. Immediately, her damp palm caused the glass door to move slightly and, taking advantage of her host's absence, she squeezed out onto the patio.

There was a pool here, adding colour to creamy tiles and a tracery of trellises. She could smell the mingled fragrances of oleander and jasmine, and even the heat seemed tempered by the breeze blowing off the sea.

A teak table set beneath a striped awning was laid with basket-weave place mats and a wine cooler. She noticed the cushions on the matching chairs blended with the colours of the canopy above her head.

Rafe came out of the house at that moment, sliding the door wide and startling her a little. 'Shall we eat out here?' he asked. 'Carla's just making us a salad.' He moved further onto the patio, revealing the bottle he was carrying. 'Will you have a glass of wine?'

Lily was reluctant, but it would have seemed churlish to refuse. 'Just a little,' she said and he turned back into the house, only to re-emerge moments later with two glasses.

Rafe set the glasses on the table and expertly extracted the cork from the bottle. 'I think Chablis is the perfect accompaniment to a salad, don't you?'

Lily pulled a wry face. 'I wouldn't know,' she con-

fessed honestly. 'My father doesn't drink alcohol and
we never have wine in the house.'

Rafe nodded and, watching him, Lily wondered
when she'd stopped thinking of him as *Mr* Oliveira.
Somewhere between Mac's Bar and here, she reflected ruefully. She hoped she wouldn't regret it.

The woman who served their meal was small and
plump and jolly. Rafe introduced her and she gave
Lily a generous, if slightly curious, smile. 'Try and
persuade him to eat something, will you, Ms Fielding,' she said. 'He doesn't eat at all when he's on
his own.'

'That is an exaggeration,' said Rafe tolerantly,
and Carla pulled a face. They were obviously good
friends as well as employer and employee.

'Enjoy your lunch,' she said, twitching a napkin
in the basket of rolls she'd laid beside the dish of
salad. Then, with another thoughtful look at Lily,
she left them to it.

'I suggest we help ourselves,' said Rafe, adding a
little more wine to his glass. 'Is this all right for you?'

'It's amazing,' she said, wondering how Carla
could have produced such a delicious meal at short
notice. A fresh lobster salad and warm crusty rolls
with butter. What could be nicer?

Despite being aware that Rafe spent more time
watching her than eating his food, Lily enjoyed the
meal. She even drank two glasses of wine before
putting her napkin aside and lying back in her chair,
replete.

Rafe arched his dark brows enquiringly, and Lily gave a satisfied nod. Then, looking at his plate, 'But you've hardly eaten a thing.'

'I will eat later,' said Rafe, though Lily had the feeling he probably wouldn't.

'You should,' she said, regarding him with some concern, and Rafe gave a mocking smile.

'Why should you care?' he countered, and a hint of colour invaded her throat.

'Tell me why you chose to come to Orchid Cay,' she said, changing the subject. 'Why not—Jamaica or Barbados? One of the larger islands?'

Rafe shrugged. 'I bought a house. This house. And some land.' He pushed back his chair. 'Come. There is something I would like you to see.'

Lily made a doubtful gesture. 'I don't really have time.'

But she couldn't deny she was curious and when he said, 'Five minutes,' she gave in.

Despite his frown, she insisted on taking her handbag with her, ready for leaving. But, as they crossed the marble hall, a man emerged from the back of the house and came towards them.

He was tall and well-built in appearance, with greying dark hair and blue eyes, and a face that had evidently taken some knocks. But it was a kindly face and Lily thought how lucky Rafe was to have such pleasant people working for him.

If indeed the man was an employee.

It appeared he was.

'Oh, hey, Mr Oliveira,' he said, 'do you have a minute?'

Rafe's lips tightened. 'Is it urgent?'

The man nodded. 'I think so.'

'Okay.' Rafe turned to Lily. 'This is my assistant, Steve Bellamy,' he said. 'Will you excuse me for a moment?'

'Of course.' Although Lily was unhappily aware that it was already approaching three o'clock. 'Um... perhaps I could use the bathroom?'

Rafe showed her where the restroom opened off the lobby where they had first entered the house and then re-joined Steve, who was waiting in his study.

'I thought you'd be interested to know who that guy was who was tailing you the other day,' he said, a little smugly. 'His name is Sawyer, and he's employed by a detective agency in New York.'

'New York?' Rafe stared at him. 'So do you know who employed him?'

'Oh, yes.' Steve nodded in satisfaction. 'He was employed by a Mrs Frances.'

'Mrs *Frances*? I don't know anyone called Mrs Frances.'

'Yeah, you do.' Steve nodded again. 'Didn't you tell me that your ex was called Sarah *Frances* Hilton before you got married?'

The restroom was as elegantly equipped as the rest of the house. Lily used the facilities, pulled a face at her tangled hair and emerged to find Rafe waiting for her outside.

When he started up the stairs, Lily hesitated. Yet what did she expect him to do? she chided herself impatiently. He was hardly likely to be taking her to his bedroom to make mad passionate love to her.

However tantalising a scenario that might be.

'Are you coming?'

Rafe was standing on the galleried landing looking down at her now, and Lily felt her awareness of him move up another notch. He needed a shave, she thought, her breath hitching. But the truth was, the hint of stubble on his jaw only added to his dark appeal.

'The house is very Spanish, isn't it?' she said as she mounted the stairs, trying to distract herself.

'I hesitate to remind you that I am half Spanish,' he remarked drily as she reached the landing. 'Do you like it? I designed some of the furnishings myself.'

'It's—beautiful.' Lily looked about her, noticing the cream panelled walls and the tiny statues of the saints that occupied any available niche. She wrapped her arms about her midriff in an unknowingly protective gesture. 'And you live here alone?'

Rafe's lips twisted. 'I do not have a mistress hidden in the basement, if that is what you mean,' he responded. 'Is that what you are hinting at?'

'Perhaps.' Lily was honest. Then, with some audacity, 'You're a very attractive—older—man.'

'Ah. An older man, *sí*.'

She was right, but that didn't stop his eyes from lingering on the dusky hint of cleavage visible in the neckline of her shirt.

'I told you about my wife, did I not?' He thought the irony of what Steve Bellamy had just relayed to him was pertinent. His lips twisted. 'I am in no hurry to put another woman in her place.'

'She was your first wife?'

'My only wife,' Rafe agreed, deciding this was getting far too heavy. He indicated the corridor that led off to their left. '*Vene, niña!* We are wasting time.'

Despite some lingering misgivings, Lily followed Rafe along a wide arched corridor where louvred windows were pushed wide to the warm air outside. She could smell the flowers, see the branches of a jacaranda swaying in the languid breeze and hear the sound of the waves as they broke on the rocks below.

'You evidently don't mind the heat,' said Lily, indicating the open windows, and Rafe gave her a lazy grin.

'When I was a boy, staying with my grandfather in Havana, I ran around naked half the time. There was no air conditioning in my grandfather's house.'

It was an image Lily chose not to linger on, and she was almost relieved when they reached the double doors that marked the end of the corridor. Rafe pushed both doors open, and then allowed her to precede him into the room beyond.

Lily's first uneasy thought was that it was a bedroom. Rafe's bedroom, perhaps, judging by the distinctly masculine coverlet on the huge bed and the sombrely painted wall behind it.

The heavy furniture too spoke of a man's influence, a polished wood tallboy and the inlaid marquetry of a square desk revealing its dual usage.

But, almost immediately, her eyes were drawn to the windows that curved round three sides of the apartment. And the view from those long windows was stunning, taking in at least half the island's coastline in an impressive sweep.

'Oh, my God!' she whispered and, although her first steps had been tentative, now Lily hurried across the room to stare incredulously at the curve of the bay.

To her left, she could see the roofs of Coral Key while, to her right, the cliffs overlooking the bay where she and her father lived were visible. Further out, the end of a rocky promontory shimmered in the haze.

'Amazing view, is it not?' murmured Rafe, giving in to the urge to stand beside her and share her enjoyment. It pleased him that she had known at once why he had brought her here.

'It's fantastic,' she agreed, suddenly aware that he had closed the door and that his bare arm was only inches from hers. Goosebumps prickled over her as his insistent gaze burned her skin. He wanted her to look at him, she knew, and it was almost impossible to resist.

FREE Merchandise and a Cash Reward† are 'in the Cards' for you!

Dear Reader,

We're giving away FREE MERCHANDISE and a CASH REWARD!

Seriously, we'd like to reward you for reading this novel by giving you **FREE MERCHANDISE** worth over **$20** retail plus a CASH REWARD! And no purchase is necessary!

You see the Jack of Hearts sticker above? Paste that sticker in the box on the Free Merchandise Voucher inside. Return the Voucher today... and we'll send you Free Merchandise plus a Cash Reward!

Thanks again for reading one of our novels—and enjoy your Free Merchandise and Cash Reward with our compliments!

Pam Powers

Pam Powers

P.S. Look inside to see what Free Merchandise is **"in the cards"** for you!

We'd like to send you two free books like the one you are enjoying now. Your two books have a combined price of over $10 retail, but they are yours to keep absolutely FREE! We'll even send you 2 wonderful surprise gifts and a Cash Reward†. You can't lose!

REMEMBER: Your Free Merchandise, consisting of **2 Free Books** and **2 Free Gifts**, is worth over **$20** retail! Plus we'll send you a **Cash Reward** (it's a dollar) which is really the icing on the cake because it's in addition to your FREE Merchandise! No purchase is necessary, so please send for your Free Merchandise today.

Get TWO FREE GIFTS!

We'll also send you 2 wonderful FREE GIFTS (worth about $10 retail), in addition to your 2 Free books and Cash Reward!

Visit us at:
www.ReaderService.com

Books received may not be as shown.

YOUR FREE MERCHANDISE INCLUDES...
2 FREE Books **AND** 2 FREE Mystery Gifts
PLUS you'll get a Cash Reward†

Detach card and mail today. No stamp needed. ▼

© 2016 HARLEQUIN ENTERPRISES LIMITED. ® and ™ are trademarks owned and used by the trademark owner and/or its licensee. Printed in the U.S.A.

FREE MERCHANDISE VOUCHER

Please send my Free Merchandise, consisting of
2 Free Books and **2 Free Mystery Gifts** PLUS my
Cash Reward. I understand that I am under no
obligation to buy anything, as explained
on the back of this card.

❏ I prefer the regular-print edition
106/306 HDL GLXA

❏ I prefer the larger-print edition
176/376 HDL GLXA

Please Print

FIRST NAME

LAST NAME

ADDRESS

APT.#   CITY

STATE/PROV.   ZIP/POSTAL CODE

Offer limited to one per household and not applicable to series that subscriber is currently receiving.
Your Privacy—The Reader Service is committed to protecting your privacy. Our Privacy Policy is available online at www.ReaderService.com or upon request from the Reader Service. We make a portion of our mailing list available to reputable third parties that offer products we believe may interest you. If you prefer that we not exchange your name with third parties, or if you wish to clarify or modify your communication preferences, please visit us at www.ReaderService.com/consumerschoice or write to us at Reader Service Preference Service, P.O. Box 9062, Buffalo, NY 14240-9062. Include your complete name and address.

NO PURCHASE NECESSARY!

P-N16-FMC15

READER SERVICE—Here's how it works:

Accepting your 2 free Harlequin Presents® books, 2 free gifts (gifts valued at approximately $10.00) and cash reward (†Cash reward available only until February 28, 2017) places you under no obligation to buy anything. You may keep the books, gifts and cash reward and return the shipping statement marked "cancel." If you do not cancel, about a month later we'll send you 6 additional books and bill you just $4.30 each for the regular-print edition or $5.30 each for the larger-print edition in the U.S. or $5.24 each for the regular-print edition or $5.74 each for the larger-print edition in Canada. That is a savings of at least 12% off the cover price. It's quite a bargain! Shipping and handling is just 50¢ per book in the U.S. and 75¢ per book in Canada.* You may cancel at any time, but if you choose to continue, every month we'll send you 6 more books, which you may either purchase at the discount price plus shipping and handling or return to us and cancel your subscription. *Terms and prices subject to change without notice. Prices do not include applicable taxes. Sales tax applicable in N.Y. Canadian residents will be charged applicable taxes. Offer not valid in Quebec. Books received may not be as shown. All orders subject to approval. Credit or debit balances in a customer's account(s) may be offset by any other outstanding balance owed by or to the customer. Please allow 4 to 6 weeks for delivery. Offer available while quantities last.

▲ If offer card is missing write to: Reader Service, P.O. Box 1867, Buffalo, NY 14240-1867 or visit www.ReaderService.com ▲

BUSINESS REPLY MAIL
FIRST-CLASS MAIL   PERMIT NO. 717   BUFFALO, NY

POSTAGE WILL BE PAID BY ADDRESSEE

READER SERVICE
PO BOX 1867
BUFFALO NY 14240-9952

NO POSTAGE
NECESSARY
IF MAILED
IN THE
UNITED STATES

But, to her relief, he turned aside and opened sliding windows onto a balcony. Filmy white curtains billowed as he stepped outside and went to rest his hands on the wrought iron rail.

She badly wanted to join him, to feel again the thrill of awareness she'd felt when he'd been standing beside her. But, glancing at the bed behind her, she was afraid she knew exactly where that might lead.

Instead, she moved away from the windows, taking in the appointments of the room with interested eyes. There was a switch beside the bed marked 'TV' and, seeing that Rafe was still on the balcony, Lily couldn't resist experimenting.

To her amazement, a huge screen rose from the baseboard at the foot of the bed and then disappeared again at the flick of another switch. Amazing!

'Having fun?' enquired her host and Lily realised that while she'd been watching the television screen returning to its resting place, Rafe had come in from the balcony and was watching her.

'I was curious,' she admitted. 'Do you mind?'

'Well, I can think of other uses for that bed,' Rafe remarked only half humorously, and then despised himself for allowing his libido to govern his words.

Lily was suddenly out of breath and not thinking very clearly, which was why her, 'I suppose I can think of other things too,' wasn't quite inaudible enough.

'Can you?' Rafe was nearer than she'd thought, the raw masculine scent of his body enveloping her in a sensual haze. 'So tell me,' he invited, not altogether sensibly, 'what did you have in mind?'

'Oh—' Lily struggled for air. 'You know: rest, sleep, stuff like that,' she muttered, not very convincingly.

'Is that all?' Rafe's tone was husky. She flinched instinctively when he put out his hand and wound a strand of her sun-streaked hair around his finger. 'I do not believe you when you tell me that all you can think of doing in this bed is resting or sleeping. Unless you have no imagination at all.'

Lily was stung by his gentle mockery. 'Of course I have an imagination,' she said, though it was hard to stay focused when just being this close to him was causing feathery shivers to attack her spine. 'I'm not stupid, Mr Oliveira. But…sex isn't a usual part of my vocabulary.'

'Whereas it is mine?' suggested Rafe, his tone hardening.

'I didn't say that.' Lily made a half-hearted attempt to use both hands to smooth her hair against her nape and then abandoned the effort. She shifted uneasily. 'It's awfully warm in here, isn't it?'

Rafe regarded her without sympathy. 'No warmer now than it was before.' He scowled. 'Are you afraid of being here alone with me?'

'Yes. No!' Lily shook her head helplessly. 'This is silly.' She cast a look up at him, half threatened by his anger. 'Oh, God, I don't know what you want me to say.'

'I suppose what I wanted you to say was that you were thinking of making love with me rather than resting and sleeping,' he remarked tersely, and then instantly regretted his words.

He'd sworn not to get involved with her, with anyone. Yet here he was, having brought a young—desirable—woman to his home, blaming her for his own uncontrollable attraction.

He moved abruptly away, sweeping back his own hair with an impatient hand. '*Lo siento*. I'm sorry,' he added with blatant self-mockery. 'I regret my imagination is far too acute.'

Lily stared at him, trying to take in what he was saying. 'You do remember you…told me to stay away from you,' she reminded him softly. 'You actually said it would be better if we didn't see one another again.'

'I lied.' Rafe was honest. 'And I believe what I actually said was that I might not be so generous next time.' He shrugged. '*De nada*. It does not matter.' He gave a small twisted smile. 'Come, I will take you back to Orchid Cay.'

'Wait.'

As he started to turn away, Lily laid a tentative hand on his bare arm. His skin was roughened by a light covering of dark hair, and there was something infinitely personal about touching him like this.

Heat enveloped her, heat and a melting sensation in her lower body. His magnetism reached out to her like the raw warmth of an open fire. It ignited a need inside her, a need she'd never felt before.

'What did you mean?' she asked, acting on impulse. 'Did you change your mind? Did you want to see me again?' She took an uneven breath. 'Is this the real reason you brought me here?'

His reaction was violent. '*Dios*, no!' he exclaimed savagely. He snatched his arm out of her grasp and stared at her with dark angry eyes. '*Mierda*, I brought you here to see the view. Nothing more.'

And *por favor Dios*, she would believe him.

'Well, I'm only trying to understand why you thought we shouldn't see one another again,' said Lily steadily, even though her pulse was racing.

'*Qué?*' Rafe swore. 'You are not that naïve, Lily.' He cradled the back of his neck with both hands as he moved his head from side to side. 'You know as well as I do that I am too old for you. You are—what? Twenty-two? Twenty-three?'

'Twenty-four, actually,' Lily corrected him. 'If you're not attracted to me, you don't have to make silly excuses.'

'Silly excuses?' Rafe groaned. 'I brought you to my home because I enjoy your company, Lily. Because, as unlikely as it might seem, you make me believe there is life after self-destruction.'

'Self-destruction?' Lily blinked. 'Whose self-destruction?'

'Mine, *por supuesto*,' said Rafe harshly, closing his eyes against the look of confusion on her face. 'Do not look at me like that. I am not suicidal, *querida*. But—' His lids flickered open again and he surveyed her with a rueful resignation. 'I cannot deny it has been a tough couple of years.'

'Oh, Rafe—'

Lily had no idea if what she was about to do was either right or sensible. Acting purely on instinct, she closed the space between them and wrapped her arms about his waist.

Then, with her face pressed to the solid warmth of his chest, she whispered, 'I'm sorry if I've said or done anything to make you think I didn't want to come here.' She tilted her head and looked up at him. 'I did. I truly did. Whether I'm too young for you or not, I am attracted to you.'

CHAPTER ELEVEN

RAFE STIRRED BUT he made no move to return her embrace, even though the sensuous warmth of her slim body pressed close to his was doing crazy things to his equilibrium. Her warm breath mingled with the tantalising scent of her body, a delicate flowery fragrance that he remembered from the last time he'd touched her.

And, remembering that occasion, he felt his arousal harden against the soft curve of her stomach. *Dios*, he wanted her, he thought unsteadily. He couldn't ever remember wanting a woman more.

But she wasn't a woman, he reminded himself; she was a girl, however much she might deny it. She was totally inexperienced when it came to men like him and he had to keep his head.

'Lily,' he groaned, struggling for restraint. 'You do not know what you are doing.'

Lily acknowledged that she probably didn't. But she couldn't deny the excitement of knowing he wanted her. And in knowing, allowing her own excitement to emerge.

She withdrew her hands from his back and allowed them to slide sinuously up his chest. With what Rafe recognised as an innate sensuality, she cupped his neck, her nails grazing his skin. 'What's wrong?' she asked huskily, bestowing a soft kiss at the corner of his mouth. 'Have I shocked you now?' A smile touched her lips. 'Well, that's a first.'

She'd shocked herself, she realised. Who would have thought she could be so provocative? With increasing confidence, she allowed her lips to brush his again, revelling in the pleasure it gave her.

Rafe groaned. He knew he'd regret what he was about to do, but he couldn't resist her. Not in this mood, not when she was bringing him so close to the edge.

Bringing his hands up to her shoulders, he pushed the neckline of her sweater aside with his thumbs and bent to brush his mouth over her bare shoulder.

She tasted of woman, of heat, of mindless ecstasy. There was a pulse fluttering in her throat, its erratic beat matching his own. Her skin was slightly damp, deliciously so, tempting him to suck the soft flesh into his mouth.

He was desperate to see more of her. His hands moved up to peel her sweater over her breasts. The gentle cleft between them incited his hunger and he paused a moment to taste her again.

As he licked the dusky hollow, his roughening jaw scraping her tender flesh, she trembled. But she didn't attempt to stop him. She simply took a shaky breath when he unclipped her bra to expose her swollen breasts.

Madrena de Dios, he groaned silently, she was delicious, her nipple pebbling automatically against his palm. Her vulnerability both delighted him and shamed him, but that didn't stop him from finally taking possession of her mouth.

Which was when all coherent thought ceased. Later, he chided himself that he should have remembered how desirably sexy she'd been that day in the park. It had been a battle then to keep his head when he was with her. Here, in the quiet intimacy of his bedroom, he had no weapon to defend himself against her sensual appeal.

Her mouth opened beneath his, sweet and also hotly passionate. If he was out of control, she was too. The tip of her tongue tangled with his as he thrust between her lips. And, like a swimmer caught in a treacherous current, he was immediately swept out of his depth.

It was a tide of feeling he didn't even try to fight against. With her hands twined in the damp hair at the back of his neck and her slender body moulded to his, there was no way he could hide what she was doing to him.

His erection was hard against her stomach and, as she came up on her toes to accommodate him, he ground his hips against her in an effort to ease his aching shaft.

Lily's head swam. Rafe's hands were behind her

now, cupping her bottom and lifting her against his sex. Her body felt light, weightless, yet her bones continued to support her, even though she was sure they'd turned to jelly beneath her.

Her whole being was alive to his lovemaking. She could feel every intimate angle of his body, the burning heat of his arousal pulsing hotly against her.

He suckled her breast, his teeth grazing her nipple as he took the swollen nub into his mouth. The stubble on his chin was rough but she revelled in the sensation, even though it caused a red welt to appear upon her skin.

'I am so sorry,' he said huskily, but she wouldn't let him draw back. Holding his head against her, she welcomed the sweet pain as he lost control.

Rafe's hands were on her hips now, feeling the delicate bones moving beneath her skin. When his fingers slipped inside her shorts, warm globes of flesh spilled into his hands, smooth and soft and silky. With a catch in his breath, he thrust her offending shorts and lacy underwear down to the tops of her legs.

'This is so much better,' he said thickly, looking down at the curls of brown-streaked hair just visible above the wedge of cotton and silk. 'You are so beautiful.'

Watching him, Lily felt as if her heart was going to burst out of her chest, it was beating so madly. Then, when his mouth sought hers again, she burrowed beneath his shirt to spread her palms against the taut muscles of his chest.

Rafe groaned in agony. Releasing her mouth for only a moment, he tore his shirt over his head. The intimacy of his bare torso pressed against her breasts left Lily breathless, and she swayed a little dizzily as a sensuous tension held her in its grip.

'*Te deseo*. I want you,' he muttered, tossing his shirt aside. 'You have no idea how much I want you.'

'I think I do,' Lily whispered, amazed that she felt no shame in standing there virtually naked in front of him. She ran an experimental finger over the hard ridge that bulged against his zip. 'Can I see?'

Rafe gazed down at her with smouldering eyes. With fingers that shook a little, he unfastened the button at the waist of his pants and tore his zip open. Then he shoved the cargo pants down around his ankles, his erection belling against the front of dark green silk boxers.

He heard her sudden intake of breath as she looked at him, took an intake of breath of his own when she stroked him through the fine cloth. '*Querida,*' he muttered hoarsely, his control virtually non-existent. But she only laid a finger across his lips, silencing his protest.

There was a tiny bead of moisture on the thick head of his erection and, although Lily had never done such a thing before, she bent and removed it with her tongue.

'*Dios,*' Rafe groaned, shuddering from the innocent stimulation. 'Do you want me to lose all self-respect?'

Lily lifted her head and looked at him. Then, quite deliberately, she lifted her leg and caressed his calf with the sole of her foot.

'I want you,' she said huskily, aware of how she was opening herself to him.

And Rafe paused only long enough to push her shorts down her legs before swinging her up into his arms.

Her legs came about his waist as he lifted her and when they tumbled onto his bed he could feel her heat melting his doubts away. When he pushed his hand down between them, her essence was wet upon his fingers and he gently eased between the folds of flesh to find its pulsing source.

Lily moaned as he caressed her. Sensations she'd never felt before were causing her body to writhe and arch beneath him. She realised that, despite her boast of experience, she'd never known the kind of emotions Rafe was arousing. And when a sudden climax took her by surprise she could only cling to him in wild abandon.

His erection was pressed against her stomach now, hot and heavy, and Rafe was licking his way from nipples wet from his attention to where her breath escaped in jerky gasps.

His teeth grazed her lips, bit into the tender skin on the inside of her mouth, took possession. He kissed her hotly, hungrily, the heat of his tongue exploring and expanding her need.

Lily had thought she had experienced the demands of passion, but she was realising Rafe had only just begun.

She could scarcely breathe as he moved over her. 'Oh, please,' she said on a whimper, her hands buried in his hair now, her nails digging desperately into his scalp. 'Please, Rafe, you're killing me.'

'You are sure this is what you want?' asked Rafe unsteadily, wondering what he'd do if she'd changed her mind. Go quietly mad, he thought. Or perhaps not so quietly. He'd be tempted to howl his frustration to the moon.

'I'm sure,' Lily panted as he tugged an inch of soft flesh into his mouth, leaving his mark on her throat. 'I want you. I do.'

'I believe you,' Rafe told her roughly, drawing back to part her legs. But she couldn't deny a quiver of apprehension as he pushed urgently into her slick core.

She sucked in a breath as he invaded her body. She'd thought she was ready, but nothing could have prepared her for Rafe's size and strength. Powerful muscles invaded moist flesh and she trembled violently. But her reaction was only a forerunner of what was to come.

She felt Rafe's fingers spreading her wider, felt him massaging the nub of her womanhood with his thumb. Another incredible wave of feeling came over her and she was swept up by the sensation. And, as it enveloped her, she lost herself completely once again.

'Es bien?' Rafe breathed against her throat, his muscles taut with the effort of controlling himself, and Lily nodded.

'But you—you haven't—' she began unsteadily, and he made a strangled sound in his throat.

'But I will,' he assured her fervently, realising that nothing was surer. And, unable to wait any longer, he drew back before pressing with increased urgency into her.

Lily was amazed to find her body responding once more to his lovemaking. As he moved with a wild and hungry abandon, she felt her own arousal stirring again. Her legs came around his waist and she arched herself against him as she met his rhythm and matched it with her own.

Rafe was sure he couldn't get any deeper. And when her muscles clenched around him, drenching him in the sweetness of her essence, he lost all restraint.

The frenzy of her orgasm left her weak and clinging to him. And his own convulsions lasted long after he'd spilled his seed inside her, the heady call of nirvana leaving his body pulsing hotly against her womb.

It was the sound of raised voices that awakened her.

Lily opened her eyes to find the room was filling with the shadows of late afternoon. The window that opened onto the balcony was still ajar and the sheer drapes billowed lazily. And when she propped herself up on her elbows she could see a yacht out on the water, its white sails stark against the blue.

She knew immediately where she was, of course. In Rafe's bed in Rafe's house, looking out at the view that had so delighted her a couple of hours ago.

She glanced about her, but she was alone in the huge bed. Rafe had evidently not fallen asleep as she had. Did that mean he was used to spending mindless afternoons making love?

Probably, she conceded uneasily, finding it hard to believe that what had happened had been as earth-shattering to him as it had been to her.

Her cheeks burned suddenly as she remembered how shamelessly she'd behaved. Had she really invited him to make love to her instead of accepting his offer to take her back to Orchid Cay? He'd been prepared to do the right thing and she'd stopped him. Whatever interpretation she put on Rafe's actions in the future, she had been equally to blame.

Her father would be horrified if he ever found out how she'd spent the afternoon. It was to be hoped that Ray Myers hadn't rung home looking for her and alerted Reverend Fielding to his daughter's absence.

All the same, she could imagine Ray's outrage when she didn't return to the agency. Was he petty enough to report that she'd gone off with the other man?

Of course, he couldn't know for sure where she was, but he was bound to speculate. Rafe hadn't returned to the restaurant and in Ray's eyes the facts would speak for themselves.

A sheet was all that covered her and, on impulse, she gathered a handful and pressed her face into the soft folds. The sheet smelt of silk and heat and the unmistakable scent of Rafe's body. And sex, she acknowledged tremulously. Raw, uninhibited sex.

The voices came again, nearer this time, and she stiffened. The sound appeared to be coming from the corridor outside Rafe's suite of rooms. It wasn't Rafe's voice. It was two women talking together. But, of course, she didn't recognise either of the voices.

She had to get up, she thought guiltily. She had to get up and get her clothes on before whoever it was decided to come into the room. She'd be so embarrassed if anyone found her like this. Without any clothes; without any hiding place; without any dignity.

She realised suddenly that the voices had gone silent. Breathing a sigh of relief, Lily took her chance and put a tentative leg over the side of the bed. Gathering up her scattered clothes, she realised she needed the bathroom. It might be a good idea to get dressed in there as well.

She had started across the carpeted floor when someone tapped at the door behind her. Panic gripped her and, dropping her clothes again, she snatched up the sheet from the bed and dragged it sarong-wise around her naked form.

Before she could speak, the door opened and a

maid appeared. 'Oh, Ms—Fielding,' she said in some confusion. 'I thought you'd gone.'

Lily moistened her lips. 'You did?'

'Yes, ma'am.' The girl hesitated. 'When Mr Oliveira left for Orchid Cay, I thought you had gone with him.'

Lily swallowed. 'Mr Oliveira has gone into town?' she exclaimed weakly, and the maid nodded.

'Yes, ma'am.' She paused and then, as if feeling that something more was needed, she added, 'Mr Bellamy came to fetch him.'

'Mr Bellamy?'

Lily knew she sounded bewildered but she couldn't help it, and the maid looked embarrassed now.

'I think they've gone to see Mrs Oliveira,' she declared as her colour deepened. 'I know I heard Mr Bellamy mention Mrs Oliveira's name.'

Lily caught her breath. 'I see.'

'But I'm sure Perez can take you home, if you don't want to wait until they come back,' murmured the girl awkwardly. 'I can ask him, if you like.'

'Perez?' Lily didn't recognise the name.

'He works for Mr Oliveira,' explained the maid. 'If you'll come downstairs when you've got—when you're ready, I'll speak to Carla about it.'

Lily was stunned. She was fairly sure the other girl had been about to say *When you've got your clothes on*, but she'd had the decency to change it at the last minute.

'And when did Mr Oliveira leave?' asked Lily tensely.

'He left about an hour ago,' replied the girl unhappily. She paused, evidently wishing she'd never entered the room. 'Is there anything you need?'

'I—no.'

Lily wondered if she could believe her. It seemed incredible that Rafe would leave her here to go and see his ex-wife.

In the silence that followed the maid's departure, Lily had to press her hand over her mouth to silence the sudden sob that rose in her throat. Oh, God, she felt so ashamed. She didn't think she'd ever felt so devastated in her life.

She dressed quickly in the bathroom, abandoning any thought of taking a shower in the cream and gold luxury she found there.

Then, after tugging a comb through the tangled mass of her hair, hair that Rafe had said he loved burying his face in, she secured it in a ponytail. It didn't matter what anyone thought of her now, she told herself. The damage was done.

It was getting dark by the time she hurried along the corridor to the head of the stairs. She realised suddenly that it was after six o'clock. Dear God, her father would be starting to get worried. She was usually home from the agency long before now.

Lamps had been lit in the hall, uplighters that cast mellow shadows over the flowers and statuary she'd admired that afternoon.

What a difference a few hours could make, she thought bitterly. But at least it had taught her a salutary lesson. That, despite everything, despite the way she had behaved towards Lily, Laura Mathews had been right.

Rafe Oliveira was not a man to trust.

CHAPTER TWELVE

IT WAS AFTER seven by the time Rafe got back to Orchid Point.

He pulled the Lexus to a halt beside the garages only seconds before Steve Bellamy drew in behind him. The two men got out of their respective cars, and for once Steve looked slightly shamefaced.

'I'm sorry, Mr Oliveira,' he muttered apologetically. 'I could have sworn it was her.'

'Well, *sí*, it might have been.' Rafe wasn't taking anything for granted. 'And you were right to be suspicious after identifying Sawyer.'

'All the same...'

'Relax,' Rafe advised him as they headed for the house. 'Just keep your eyes and ears open. If she is on the island, she is bound to come here.'

'You think?'

'Do you not think the same?' Rafe pulled a face at him. 'Hey, it is not what I want,' he reminded his assistant drily. 'But who knows what she might try next?'

'So what are you going to do?'

Rafe's face relaxed into a grin. 'Me? Oh, I am going to get changed and then go and find a certain young lady and apologise for abandoning her,' he said cheerfully. 'I only hope she will understand when I tell her I have been looking for my ex-wife.'

Steve's brows arched. 'Am I allowed to ask who she is?' He paused. 'Did I tell you Ms Mathews was absolutely furious when I got to the bar?'

'You have mentioned it once or twice,' said Rafe, tongue in cheek, and Steve pulled a wry face.

'Well, it's true. Myers was doing his best to placate her, but I think she wants your blood.'

'She wants my money,' Rafe corrected him flatly. 'Or rather her Daddy does. He has evidently given her the impression that I cannot resist a beautiful woman and that if she plays her cards right I will agree to anything she asks.'

'But—' Steve gave his employer an awkward look. 'I mean—that's not true. The bit about you and other women.' He knew better than anyone that his employer hadn't seen another woman since they'd left New York months ago.

'Thanks.' Rafe patted his shoulder gratefully. 'And, just for the record, Ms Fielding's name is Lily. Her father is the Anglican minister I was telling you about.'

'An Anglican minister's daughter?' Steve arched a doubtful brow. 'Is that wise?'

'Probably not, but she fascinates me,' said Rafe ruefully. 'I just hope she believes me when I tell her where I have been. With Laura doing her best to ruin my reputation and Sarah plotting heaven knows what, do I really stand a chance?'

Steve glanced Rafe's way again as they entered the house. It was easier to see his expression in the artificial light and he frowned. 'The Mathews woman mentioned her, as it happens. She said she'd barged in on your lunch date, and Myers backed her up.'

'It was not a lunch date,' retorted Rafe impatiently. 'I agreed to have a drink with Laura, that was all. I was grateful for the reprieve.'

Steve arched an enquiring brow. 'You don't find Ms Mathews fascinating?' he asked drily and Rafe pulled a wry face.

'She certainly thinks she has got what it takes,' he conceded. 'But if you mean: does she attract me? I can honestly say no. Women like her leave me cold.'

Steve absorbed this. 'I suppose she is a bit like the first Mrs Oliveira, isn't she?'

Rafe stifled a laugh. 'Hell, no.' He saw Carla coming towards him and added in an undertone, 'That woman is in a class by herself.'

Steve grinned, but then the frown on the housekeeper's face caused both men to look at her enquiringly. 'Is something wrong?' Rafe asked quickly. 'Do not tell me Ms Fielding got tired of waiting and went home.'

Carla looked discomfited. 'Well, she has gone, Mr Oliveira.' And, at his impatient oath, she added, 'But I don't think it was because she got tired of waiting.'

She paused and then added unhappily, 'One of the maids told her you'd gone into town with Mr Bellamy to speak to your ex-wife.' She saw Rafe's expression change and hurried on regardless. 'I don't know why she went into your suite, Mr Oliveira. I'd told her to vacuum one of the other rooms on that floor, but that's what happened.'

'*Dios!*' Rafe swore. He could imagine what Lily must be thinking.

'When she—well, when Ms Fielding came downstairs,' Carla continued apologetically, 'she insisted on leaving. I tried to tell her that you'd probably be back soon, but she'd have none of it.'

'*Mierda!*' Rafe stared at her disbelievingly. 'I do not believe this! Could you not have explained the situation?'

'I didn't think you'd want me discussing your ex-wife with—well, with a virtual stranger,' said Carla defensively. 'Evidently I made a mistake.'

'Yes, you did,' muttered Rafe angrily. And then, realising he shouldn't blame Carla for his own mistake, he added in some contrition, 'I am sorry. That was uncalled for. It was my mistake. I just hope Ms Fielding understands my dilemma.'

Lily was already sitting at the table when her father came to join her. The meal—a chilled consommé of vegetables followed by pulled pork, cooked with cinnamon and brown sugar—was delayed, thanks to Lily's late return.

But, as her father had been working in his study when she arrived home, she hoped he hadn't noticed the time.

She was soon disabused of that notion, however.

'Where have you been?' he asked, making no attempt to pick up his spoon. 'I've had Myers on the phone at least three times in the last couple of hours. He's been worried about you and, frankly, so have I.'

Lily didn't know how to answer him. 'I… I'm sorry,' she said at last. 'I got…held up.'

'By whom?' her father enquired coolly. 'According to Myers, you haven't even shown your face at the agency since lunch.'

Lily expelled a careful breath. 'I… I was busy,' she muttered, silently cursing Ray Myers for putting her in this position. 'Am I not entitled to have a life outside the agency? I'm twenty-four, Dad. Not sixteen.'

'I know.' William Fielding's expression didn't change, however. 'But you are still my daughter and I feel I have a right to know what you've been doing. This is a small island, Lily. I wouldn't like—people—to think you were out of control.'

'Out of control?'

The words were so ludicrous, and yet so apt, that Lily didn't know whether to laugh or cry.

In truth, she'd been out of control for most of the afternoon, she thought. And it was true, she'd been on the verge of tears ever since that man, Perez, had driven her back to town to pick up her car. But her father knew nothing about that.

'I know I'm old-fashioned,' he went on now, and Lily tried to concentrate on what he was saying. 'But—well, I wouldn't like you to turn out like that friend of yours, Laura Mathews.'

Lily sighed. 'I won't,' she said flatly. That was one thing she could be certain about.

But her father wouldn't leave it alone. Regarding her with some suspicion, he added, 'If what I hear is true, you've spent the afternoon with Rafe Oliveira.'

Lily's face turned scarlet. 'How do you know that?'

'It's true then?' There was disappointment in his voice now. His face took on a pinched expression. 'Oh, Lily, I thought you had more sense.'

'More sense?' Lily attempted to use indignation to stave off the sense of devastation that gripped her. She strove for a defence. 'I thought you liked him.'

'I do like him.' William Fielding heaved a sigh. 'But that's not the point.'

'What is the point then?'

'How many do you need?' Her father was impatient. 'He's too old for you, for one thing. And the man has a history, Lily. If the newspapers are to be believed, he only just avoided being convicted of drug offences and who knows what else?'

'I know that.'

'You know it?' Her father caught his breath. 'How

do you know this? Who told you? Oh, I suppose it was Laura. Of course, she has her own axe to grind.'

'It was—Oliveira, actually,' said Lily quickly. She noticed she'd reverted to his surname, but she hurried on before her father could comment. 'What did you mean about Laura? How is she involved?'

'You mean she didn't tell you?' He stared at her in disbelief. 'I was sure that was why she came round here the other night. As a matter of fact, that was why I kept out of her way.'

Lily felt sick. 'Are you saying—?' She didn't want to say the words but she had to. 'Are you implying that Laura and Oliveira are—*were*—lovers?'

If she'd hoped for a swift denial, she was disappointed. 'Lovers?' said her father doubtfully. He lifted his shoulders in a helpless gesture. 'Well, they could be, I suppose. Do you think they are?'

Lily wanted to scream. 'No,' she said, trying to remain calm. 'I was asking you if that was what you'd heard.' And when he still looked confused she said frustratedly, 'Dad, you said Laura had her own axe to grind, remember?'

'Oh! Oh, I see.' Her father's expression cleared. 'Of course. Obviously you don't know what I'm talking about or you'd understand.' He paused and, to Lily's distress, he picked up a spoon and took a mouthful of his soup. 'Mmm, this is good. Pour me a glass of water, will you, my dear?'

Lily reached for the water jug with trembling fingers, praying she wouldn't spill liquid all over the table as she filled his glass.

But this was typically her father: create a situation and then let it stew while he attended to other matters. Didn't he realise she was desperate to hear what he had to say? Didn't he care?

'Eat up, my dear,' he advised cheerfully when Lily made no move to copy his actions. He sniffed appreciatively. 'I may grumble about Dee-Dee's beliefs, but I can't fault her cooking. Is that pulled pork? My favourite! It smells delicious.'

'I made most of the meal, Dad,' said Lily in a monotone. It was incredibly difficult not to get angry with him, but at least it was keeping other thoughts at bay.

'You did?' Her father was surprised. 'But I thought you'd been out all afternoon. When did you find the time to make a meal like this?'

Lily shook her head. 'The consommé was already made,' she said wearily. 'And Dee-Dee put the pork in the oven before she left for the day. All I had to do was cook the vegetables.'

'Very good.' William Fielding nodded agreeably. 'Well, let me compliment you, my dear. It's a long time since I've enjoyed a meal so much.'

Exactly two weeks, thought Lily grimly, but she didn't say so. Her father's absent-mindedness used to be one of the things she loved about him, but tonight it was grating on her nerves. Why didn't he tell her what he'd meant about Laura? Did it please him to keep her in suspense?

Picking up her own soup bowl, which hadn't been touched, and her father's, which was empty, Lily left the table and carried them into the kitchen. After pouring her own soup away, she dumped both dishes in the sink.

Then, propping her elbows on the edge of the basin, she cupped her chin in her hands and stared blindly through the window to the darkness outside.

She had no desire to return to the dining room. The casserole dish containing the pork and vegetables was already on the table and her father was quite capable of helping himself.

She still felt sick and her head was thumping quite badly. It hardly seemed possible that only hours before she'd considered herself the luckiest girl in the world.

Everything had gone downhill since she'd awakened to find herself alone in Oliveira's bed. But even then it had taken her some time to latch onto the fact that he'd abandoned her.

She should have known instantly what had happened; after all, he'd warned her that they had no future together days ago. Yet she'd fooled herself into thinking he didn't mean it. She'd been so bemused by his lovemaking that she hadn't believed it was all just a game to him.

It had been so humiliating when the maid had told

her that he'd gone to see his ex-wife. The girl had looked at Lily with what she was sure was pity. Had he been lying about their relationship? She could only think the worst.

Dear God!

Lily shivered. It was all her own fault. She could have refused to have lunch with him. And when he'd taken her to his house, she could have refused to get out of the car.

But she hadn't. At every turn she'd succumbed to his persuasion. And, to add insult to injury, she had been the one to initiate their lovemaking, not him.

Thank heaven her father only assumed she'd had a date with Oliveira. He had no conception of the depths to which his daughter had sunk.

What if she discovered that Oliveira had been involved with his ex-wife in New York before he came to the island? If that was so, Lily thought she'd die of humiliation. But it might explain why Laura had warned her to stay away from him. Despite the fact that Lily was sure the other girl wasn't indifferent to the man.

A shadow moved at the edge of the patio and Lily drew back from the sink, her hands falling to her sides. Someone was out there, in the garden, she thought, but she hadn't heard a car's engine. Whoever it was must have parked some distance away and walked around to the back of the house.

Oliveira!

She wished now she'd turned out the light while

she was standing there feeling sorry for herself. As it was, when he materialised out of the darkness she had no place to hide. He saw her and came to the window, tapping on the glass, indicating that she should unlock the back door and let him in. But Lily didn't move. She was frozen to the spot.

Then anger energised her. How dare he come here tonight? she thought furiously. What on earth could he want with her now?

Or was it her father he'd come to see? She wouldn't put it past him. What did he intend to do? Slip the fact that he'd spent the afternoon in bed with his daughter into the conversation?

'Open the door, Lily,' he called when she didn't move and it sounded like an order.

'Go to hell,' she mouthed silently, desperate that her father shouldn't hear and come to see what was going on.

Oliveira's scowl appeared and, leaving the window, he came to hammer on the door instead. 'I am not leaving, Lily,' he shouted harshly. 'Grow up. We need to talk.'

Lily closed her eyes despairingly. If she refused to open the door, sooner or later her father was bound to hear the noise. Oliveira was a powerful man. If he really put his mind to it, he could easily kick the door in.

'Lily?'

She opened her eyes somewhat guiltily to find her father standing in the open doorway behind her. His brows were drawn together and she guessed the decision had been taken out of her hands. 'Oh, hi, Dad,' she said, still hoping she could rescue the situation. But then Oliveira knocked again and she knew there was no escape.

'I thought I heard someone at the door,' said William Fielding impatiently. 'Goodness me, why do emergencies always happen when we're right in the middle of a meal?'

'It's not an emergency, Dad,' Lily began, but her father had already crossed the room and was reaching for the handle. Releasing the lock, he pulled the door open.

'Oh,' he said when he saw their visitor. 'Oh, it's you.' He glanced behind him at his daughter. 'Did you know who it was?'

'She knew,' Rafe answered for her, stepping into the room without waiting for an invitation. *'Buenas tardes, padre,'* he greeted the older man politely. 'Do you mind if I speak with Lily alone?'

Lily noticed that Oliveira hadn't changed his clothes since that afternoon. He was still wearing the black shirt and khaki trousers he'd worn in Mac's Bar.

A little creased now, she noticed, not wanting to remember how that had happened. But it did surprise her. He was a man, she felt, who cared about his appearance. Yet his hair was rumpled and the stubble on his jawline was more pronounced than when he'd grazed her tender skin.

However, the eyes he turned in her direction were like dark coals of fire.

The Reverend Fielding's nostrils had flared at the other man's audacity in entering his home uninvited.

'We are right in the middle of supper, Mr Oliveira,' he said tersely. 'It would be more convenient if you could speak to my daughter at some other time. Tomorrow, perhaps. She'll be at the Cartagena Charters agency in the morning, as usual. If you don't know where that is, I'd be happy to give you directions.'

'I do know where the agency is,' Rafe responded shortly, resisting the urge to tell the other man that that was where he and Lily had first met.

Had she told her father that? Or did Fielding assume they'd met the night Rafe had offered to look for her? The night, he remembered savagely, when he'd been tortured by dreams of her rising naked from the waves.

'Very well.'

Lily guessed her father thought that was the end of the discussion. He was so used to people deferring to him that it hadn't occurred to him that Oliveira might disagree.

'*Sin embargo*, I would prefer to speak with Lily tonight, if it is convenient,' Rafe said firmly, and Lily doubted he cared even if it wasn't. He turned those disturbing eyes in her direction again. 'I am sure she can afford me a few minutes of her time.'

William Fielding's mouth tightened and when he turned to his daughter, Lily knew he expected her to back him up. But she didn't know what Oliveira might say if she refused him. He looked just unpredictable enough to say anything to get his own way.

'Maybe—five minutes, Dad?' she suggested, hating the hold Oliveira had over her. She was letting her father down and she'd never done that before.

The older man regarded her distantly. 'If that's what you want, I can't stop you,' he said with evident disapproval. He glanced once more at the visitor. 'Please don't keep her too long.'

CHAPTER THIRTEEN

RAFE DIDN'T ANSWER. He was not in the mood to placate the other man or anyone else. *Nombre de Dios*, he doubted Fielding knew he had done anything wrong.

Reverend Fielding hesitated a few moments but then, when it became apparent that Rafe wasn't going to say anything more in his presence, he uttered a most uncharacteristic exclamation and walked out of the room.

He left the door ajar, however, but, to Lily's dismay, Oliveira brushed past her and went to close it. Then, turning, his shoulders resting against the panels, he regarded her with a curious mix of wariness and regret.

The silence stretched between them for several seconds and Lily's nerves were drawn as tight as violin strings. She was on the point of demanding he say what he had to say and get out when he spoke.

'I am sorry if the maid upset you,' he said unexpectedly. 'She had no right to enter the suite. Be assured, she has been—advised of that fact.'

Lily drew a tremulous breath. What was she supposed to say to that? she wondered. Did he think telling her that the maid had made a mistake in coming into the room excused him? He'd still abandoned her to go and see his ex-wife.

'It doesn't matter,' she said now, just wanting him to leave before she said something she'd regret. He'd left the villa without even stopping to take a shower or change his clothes. He was both a bastard and a liar. After all he'd said, she was filled with both bitterness and despair.

'It does matter,' Rafe contradicted her bleakly now. 'I can imagine how you must have felt.'

'Oh, really?' Lily was scornful. 'It's happened to you too, has it? Forgive me if I find that very hard to believe.'

Rafe straightened away from the door, anger simmering. What right had she to criticise him when she wouldn't even give him a chance to explain?

'I see I was right,' he said harshly. 'Although you pretend to be a woman, you act like a child! I do regret what happened. All of it. Believe me, the situation was not of my making.'

Lily turned away. She was trembling, but she was damned if she'd let him see that. 'Well, thanks for your apology, if that's what it was.' She moved towards the outer door. 'I'll tell my father you said goodbye.'

He swore then. Lily didn't understand the words but their meaning was clear enough. What she wasn't prepared for was that he should grasp her shoulders and jerk her back against him, or that he would continue to mutter imprecations, his breath hot and sensual against her neck.

Rafe hadn't intended to touch her. Indeed, when she'd made her acid little retort and turned her back on him, he'd told himself it was probably best for all concerned.

She was too young for him. That was the truth. And, in the present situation, he shouldn't risk getting her involved. But it was also true that when he was with her he had little or no control over his actions.

Even being here with her now, knowing her father was in the next room, didn't stop his thoughts from retracing the intimacies they'd shared that afternoon. And the sooner he put some distance between himself and the temptation she represented, the better.

But she'd caught her glorious hair up in a loop this evening and the heat had plastered tiny tendrils of honey-streaked silk against her nape.

Her neck was gently curved, sweetly soft and achingly vulnerable. And it was that vulnerability that drove him to haul her back against his body that was already throbbing with need.

His mouth moved against her skin, loving the scent of her, instinctively finding the sensitive nub of skin he'd bitten that afternoon.

She flinched and he guessed she'd put on this silk top, with its cowl neckline, to protect the mark from detection. But Rafe exulted in the proof of his possession, laving it with his tongue, causing her to shiver in spite of the resistance he could still feel.

'Querida,' he muttered thickly, all his previous determination to leave her foundering in the depths of his growing desire. The taste of her was like ambrosia, the sensuality she exuded drugging his senses, dragging a tortured, 'Please, do not let us quarrel, *mi corazón,'* from his lips.

'Let me go, Rafe.'

It took an enormous effort of will to say the words, but Lily told herself he deserved them. He couldn't think he could behave as he had this afternoon and then turn up here tonight as if nothing had happened.

If he thought he could seduce her into forgetting his duplicity with his beguiling words, he was very much mistaken.

His fingers dug into the bones of her shoulders and for a moment she wanted to cry with the pain. But then, with another exclamation, he twisted her round to face him, his dark face revealing his frustration.

'Qué?' he demanded roughly. 'You enjoy tormenting me, *es así*? *Bien*, two can play at that game, *querida.'* And, cupping her face between ungentle hands, he fastened his open mouth to hers.

Lily wilted when he thrust his tongue between her teeth. It was too soon, she thought weakly, her senses swimming beneath that sensual invasion. Her body remembered the afternoon only too well and, while her brain might tell her he couldn't be trusted, her resistance melted in the heat of his possession.

'Please,' she whispered against his mouth, but it was as much a plea for her own sanity as a bid for him to release her.

'You do please me, *querida*,' Rafe told her harshly, drawing back to gaze into her flushed face with hungry eyes. 'Too much for my own good.'

His thumbs found the underside of her chin, digging into the soft flesh with scant regard for the pain he was inflicting. His eyes were dark and tormented as he stared down at her.

'I came here to apologise for leaving you this afternoon, but also to tell you I could not see you again.'

'To apologise?' Lily managed a tortured laugh. 'Because you left me to renew your relationship with your ex-wife?' she demanded.

'*Mierda*, what are you saying?' Rafe drew back to look down into her accusing face.

Obviously she knew about Sarah—Carla had warned him of that. But what story had that stupid maid told her? A mangled version of events, that was for sure. In consequence, Lily had got completely the wrong idea.

Sighing, he said, 'Do you think I wanted to see my ex-wife? I had hoped never to have to see her again.'

Lily stared at him. She'd been praying that the maid was wrong. But she realised now that the man was a consummate liar, and she'd been stupid enough to get caught in his web.

'I think you should leave,' she said shakily, trying to pull away from him, and Rafe gave a bitter nod.

'I think I should too,' he muttered. This was probably not the time to try and make explanations. And yet... 'But instead you tempt me to stay.'

Lily caught her breath, torn in spite of herself. 'I don't tempt you!' she declared huskily. 'I've asked you to go, haven't I? But you're still here.'

'Perhaps you are unaware of what you are so generously offering.' Rafe was sardonic now. But he put her away from him, lifting his shoulders in a dismissive shrug. '*Sí, pequeña*, go running back to your father. If he finds out his precious daughter was with me this afternoon, he will be sure to imagine the worst.'

Lily held up her head, stung by his sarcasm. 'I wasn't a virgin,' she said tightly, but Rafe wasn't convinced.

'Physically, perhaps not.' His lips twisted. 'But in other ways...'

Lily drew a ragged breath. 'Stop treating me like a child,' she protested.

'But you are a child,' he said without malice. 'I am at fault for thinking otherwise. My only defence is that, in the past, I have always known what I wanted.' He paused. 'And, for my sins, I wanted you.'

Lily swallowed. 'So you went after me,' she stated tensely, and his eyes darkened.

'As I recall it, *querida*, you went after me,' he reminded her, angry that he couldn't get the memory out of his head. His lips twisted. 'Or do you deny that much of what happened this afternoon was a direct result of your provocation?'

Lily's face flamed with colour. 'That...that's not a very polite thing to accuse me of.'

'I am sorry.' He lifted his shoulders. 'I am not a very polite man.' He stepped back from her. 'I fear your father is right. I should not have invited you to my home. It was a—what shall I say?—a reckless thing to do.'

Lily drew in an uneven breath. Despite her feelings, she felt sick inside at the thought that he regretted what had happened. 'It's a little late to tell me that now.'

'I know.' Rafe groaned. 'But please, *querida*, do not think I took you to Orchid Point to seduce you. I did not.' He covered the space between them again and bent until his breath was hot against her parted lips. 'And you did ask me to make love with you, did you not? What can I say in my own defence? I am only human.'

Lily couldn't answer him. 'I think you should leave, Mr Oliveira.' Her breath quickened as his thumb traced the sensitive curve of her mouth. 'I don't think there's anything more to say.'

'Muy bien.' Rafe's patience gave out but, not trusting himself to go on touching her, he spread his hands wide. 'However you regard me, be aware you drive me crazy,' he told her harshly. 'And this is something I will have to live with.'

Lily took advantage of her sudden freedom to move right away from him, only stopping when her back encountered the unyielding frame of the unit behind her.

She wasn't capable of dealing with him at present. She was too vulnerable. Too aware of how it had been between them. Maybe later, when her blood pressure didn't rise every time he came near her.

Rafe sighed. 'Will you tell your father about this afternoon?'

'Why?' Lily drew an unsteady breath. 'Are you afraid of the consequences?'

'Do not be foolish.' Rafe shook his head. 'Perhaps I should tell him myself.'

Lily gasped. 'You wouldn't do that.'

'No. Because I have more respect for you than that. And I did not come here to threaten you or make the situation even more fraught.' Rafe sighed. 'I came to tell you why I had to leave so precipitately. I had had word—'

'From your ex-wife,' Lily interrupted him flatly, and he gave her a weary look.

'In a manner of speaking,' he began, but once again she broke in.

'You needn't say any more,' she said tightly. 'I'm not a fool, Mr Oliveira. I realise now what kind of man you are.'

Rafe felt his temper rising. 'I doubt that very much.'

'You underestimate me, Mr Oliveira,' she retorted, brushing past him to swing open the door.

'Please, don't let me keep you. I'm sure you have a more exciting evening in prospect.'

Rafe's jaw tightened. 'You do not know what you are talking about,' he declared coldly. 'You simply prove I am right. You are a child at heart.'

'Perhaps I am.' Lily refused to let him see that he had hurt her. Instead, she exclaimed, 'Look at you.' She waved a hand at his unkempt appearance. 'You must have been so desperate to see her that you snatched up the first shirt and trousers that came to hand.'

'These?' Rafe demanded grimly, flicking a finger at his outfit. 'This would be the shirt and trousers you so kindly helped me to take off!'

'Whatever.' Lily couldn't meet his eyes. 'I hope she appreciated your haste.'

Rafe's anger propelled him across the room again until he was standing right in front of her. 'The woman I went to see was not there,' he told her icily, putting a hand on the unit at either side of her, effectively imprisoning her. 'Did not your spies tell you that?'

'I don't have any spies.' Lily concentrated on the open vee of his shirt, where the arrowing of hair on his chest was moved tantalisingly by her breath. 'I only know what I was told by your staff.'

'And Laura Mathews?' he suggested harshly, guessing that the other girl had been involved. 'It does not occur to you that she might have an agenda of her own?'

'What agenda?' asked Lily, finding the courage to lift her head and meet his glittering gaze. 'Are you two having an affair?'

Rafe was stunned. This, after everything they'd shared. That she could think he'd go straight from her arms to those of his ex-wife was bad enough. But that she could believe that Laura, that scheming little gold-digger, might be part of the equation was simply too insulting to be borne.

Yet, feeling his body throbbing, he was disgusted to find he was still aroused. *'Por Dios,'* he swore angrily; he would conquer his need, stifle his attraction to her, once and for all.

He was about to turn away from her and leave without saying another word when the expression in her eyes arrested him. Was that apprehension he could see, or fear?

Nombre de Dios, he was appalled. She couldn't be afraid of him, could she? Or was she simply afraid of what form his reaction to her accusations might take?

He acted without thinking. Grasping her chin in his hand, he tipped her face up to his. He stared at her for a long moment. Then, almost against his will, he bent towards her, grinding his mouth against hers in one last searing kiss.

He was gone before Lily had recovered from that shattering assault on her senses. By the time she'd scrubbed a trembling hand over her mouth and turned towards the window, there was no sign of him.

But the aftermath of his kiss was evidenced in the pain that stirred deep in her belly. In the moisture she could feel pooling between her legs.

'Lily?' She was holding onto the sink, trying to quell the nausea that was rising inside her, when her father spoke from the doorway into the hall. 'My dear, are you all right?'

No, I'm dying, she thought miserably, hoping he couldn't see the way her knees were trembling. The last thing she needed right now was for her father to take a sudden interest in her welfare.

'I was watching a firefly,' she lied, hoping her face didn't give her away. She turned to look at him. 'Did you finish your supper?'

'Apart from dessert,' said William Fielding, ever pedantic. 'But you haven't eaten a thing, Lily. Don't think I haven't noticed.'

He paused and then continued stiffly, 'It's that man, isn't it? He's upset you. What did he come here for? You were only with him this afternoon. Where did he take you, by the way? Myers didn't say.'

Myers didn't know, thought Lily bitterly. She wanted to laugh, and she had to swallow the sob of hysteria that rose in her throat at his words.

'He took me to see his house,' she said, knowing the truth would come out sooner or later. 'But don't worry.' She paused. 'He...he's much too old for me.'

'Well, I'm very pleased you realise that.' Apparently reassured by her answer, her father glanced

thoughtfully over his shoulder and she guessed he
was eager to get back to either his supper or his
study.

He really was amazingly trusting when it came
to his daughter, she thought, half ashamed that she
was deceiving him in this way.

But then, just when she was beginning to breathe
more easily, he added, 'I have to say, I've nothing
against the man, personally. And I'll be interested to
hear what you thought of what he's done to the house.
Although, after the way he's treated the Mathewses,
we must be wary, mustn't we?'

Lily's tongue sought the roof of her mouth. 'The
way he's treated the Mathewses,' she echoed, daring to hope he was at last going to tell her what he'd
meant earlier.

But at that moment the telephone in William
Fielding's study rang.

'Dear me,' he said, turning away, any further con-
fidences forgotten. 'What a busy evening we're having. Excuse me, my dear. I think I ought to answer
that, don't you?'

The following morning Lily slept in.

Usually, she had her breakfast and was on her
way to the agency by nine o'clock. She had an old
Renault that she used for running about in. And just
occasionally her father borrowed it when his ancient
Lincoln refused to start.

But, as it had been the early hours of the morning

before she'd managed to fall into a troubled sleep, she was still drowsing when Dee-Dee shook her awake.

'Lily! Lily!' She opened her eyes to the sight of the housekeeper's round expectant face staring down at her. 'You all right, girl?' The woman was evidently concerned. 'I didn't even know you were still in the house.'

Lily blinked. 'Dee-Dee,' she said in some confusion. And then, as comprehension dawned, 'What time is it?'

'Time you was on your way to work,' declared Dee-Dee sagely, stepping out of the way as Lily flung back the sheet. 'Your daddy sure ain't gonna be pleased when he finds out you overslept.'

Lily sat up, swinging her legs to the side of the bed and then groaning as her head thumped in protest. If she didn't know better, she'd have said she had a hangover. Was there such a thing as an emotional hangover?

'What you been doing with yourself, girl?'

Dee-Dee fussed around her and, considering the West Indian woman was almost six feet tall and over two hundred pounds in weight, she was an intimidating presence. 'You got a headache, yeah? Dee-Dee, she got something for that.'

'It's okay, thanks.' Lily didn't trust Dee-Dee's herbal remedies. She could never be sure what she was being given.

'You been drinking?'

Dee-Dee wasn't giving up and, realising she'd

have to tell her something, Lily decided on at least a part of the truth.

'If you must know, I think Oliveira's been having an affair with Laura,' she declared tersely, choosing the least provocative option. 'Now, I've got to get dressed.'

'And you upset?'

Dee-Dee was sympathetic and Lily sighed. 'Yes, I'm upset,' she admitted. 'I know you warned me he was dangerous. And now I feel like a fool.'

'Why? You been seeing him yourself?'

Lily shrugged. She was loath to admit it to anyone, least of all Dee-Dee.

Dee-Dee's dark brows drew together as if she didn't need any confirmation. 'Who told you they was having an affair?' she demanded. 'Was it the Mathews girl?' And Lily was glad she could deny that at least. 'Don't tell me you believe anything Ray Myers says.'

'If you must know, Daddy implied as much,' said Lily wearily, refusing to mention Oliveira's ex-wife. 'Look, I really do have to get ready for work.'

'That man!' Dee-Dee snorted, referring to Lily's father. 'I don't know where he gets his ideas from. Oliveira ain't sleeping with anyone. Least of all Laura Mathews. Not that she'd turn him away if he came knocking.'

Lily, who'd been on the point of getting up from the bed, flopped back onto the mattress. 'How do you know there's not someone else?'

Dee-Dee tapped her head with a conspiratorial finger. 'How does Dee-Dee know anything?' she retorted. 'I got my sources up here. Far as I know, Oliveira ain't sharing his bed and that's a fact.'

Lily stared at her. 'Are you sure?'

'Sure I'm sure,' exclaimed the West Indian woman knowledgeably. 'As far as the Mathews girl is concerned, her father's got her running out to Orchid Point every chance he gets, trying to persuade Oliveira to rescue his sorry ass, that's all.'

'Whose sorry ass?'

Dee-Dee clicked her tongue impatiently. 'Grant Mathews's sorry ass,' she exclaimed. 'Everybody knows that man's a gambler. Since he lost all that money in Las Vegas, he's only living here thanks to Oliveira's charity.'

'I didn't know that.' Lily shook her head disbelievingly. 'I knew he'd lost a lot of money to the man.'

'The way I heard it, he didn't lose the money to Oliveira,' said Dee-Dee confusingly. Then she explained. 'The guy who took Mathews down didn't want no share in a Caribbean island. He wanted cash, see, and Oliveira bought him out.'

Lily got unsteadily to her feet. 'So that's why he came to the island.'

'Yeah. The house, the plantation, the cottages at Coral Key—not to mention Orchid Point. Pretty much everything belongs to him,' agreed Dee-Dee comfortably. 'Didn't your daddy tell you about it?'

Lily's jaw dropped. 'You mean Dad knows?'

'I'd say so.' Dee-Dee started tugging back the covers on the bed, removing the sheets for washing. 'Oliveira came to see your Daddy. Likely he wanted his blessing, so to speak. Or so your Daddy would have us believe.

'But me, I think he wanted the Reverend's advice about how this gonna go down with the people who live here. I guess he didn't realise that Grant Mathews never won no popularity contests and, from what I hear, Oliveira's doing okay.'

Lily felt hurt that her father hadn't bothered to tell her. But then, would he think it was something she needed to know?

Probably not.

Of course there was still the fact that Oliveira had walked out on her the previous afternoon to deal with. She was tempted to ask Dee-Dee her opinion about that.

Which caused another troublesome thought to stir inside her. What if Rafe hadn't been lying to her about his relationship with his ex-wife?

And, if that was so, what was she going to do about it?

CHAPTER FOURTEEN

THE NEXT FEW days passed without incident. If Lily could discount the fact that Ray was in a black mood for most of that time and barely spoke to her at all, that was.

A lot of his annoyance stemmed from the fact that Lily refused to tell him where she'd gone the afternoon she hadn't returned to the agency.

She'd apologised for her absence, had admitted she should have rung him and warned him she might not be back. But, aside from that, she'd remained silent. She had no intention of discussing Rafe with him or giving Ray the opportunity to ask her to intercede with the man on his behalf.

Lily had no idea what Rafe's decision regarding the agency might be. She knew Ray had managed to squeeze a loan from the bank to cover his immediate expenses. Which meant the group from Boston had returned home without the threat of a lawsuit hanging over Ray's head.

But he was still in debt. Goodness knew what might happen now.

Unless Rafe Oliveira came through...

But that seemed less and less likely as the days went by. She told herself she wasn't responsible if Rafe chose to withdraw any interest from the company—that he'd already decided Ray was a poor risk before she'd got involved.

Yet, the truth was, she did feel some responsibility for the worsening situation. It seemed she'd offended everybody and she didn't know what to do.

Her relationship with her father had deteriorated too. William Fielding had not taken kindly to her accusation that he'd deliberately kept the reasons for Oliveira's visit from her.

'It's nothing to do with us,' he'd maintained, when she'd tackled him about it. 'Just because Oliveira consulted me about the situation did not give me leave to discuss his affairs with all and sundry.'

'Dee-Dee knew,' Lily had muttered sulkily, but her father was adamant.

'Whether she did or not isn't important. My integrity is. Besides, if this has driven a wedge between you and Oliveira, so much the better.'

Lily had wanted to ask how he knew that a wedge had been driven between her and Rafe, but she was afraid she knew.

It seemed Dee-Dee had no compunction about spilling the beans.

A couple of days later, Ray returned from lunch looking considerably more cheerful. As he spent most lunchtimes in Mac's Bar these days, Lily wasn't altogether surprised.

But on this occasion his good humour lasted longer than it took for him to sit down at his desk and examine the schedules. Lily sensed he was hoping she would ask why he seemed so upbeat all of a sudden but, having taken several knock-backs in the past few days, she was determined not to give him a chance to criticise her again.

Eventually, Ray was forced to speak first. 'You'll never guess who I've been having a drink with,' he remarked casually, and Lily's stomach tightened automatically.

She was sure she could guess what was to come and when she didn't make any response he went on smugly, 'Rafe Oliveira.' He paused. 'You might want to congratulate me. I've just secured your job for the next couple of years.'

Lily expelled a trembling breath. 'How...how did you do that?' she asked, knowing he expected it, wondering why the relief she felt was mingled with despair.

'How do you think?' Ray smirked. 'I've persuaded him to invest in the business.' He paused for a moment and then continued a little less brashly, 'Well, he's my new partner, actually. The Oliveira Corporation is taking a nominal share in the company.'

Lily swallowed. 'How nominal?'

'Does it matter?' Ray scowled. 'Be thankful that he's prepared to invest at all.'

* * *

'You've done what?' Steve Bellamy stared at the man sitting at the other side of the desk with incredulous eyes. 'I thought you told me the business had debts it couldn't cover, that it was heading down the drain?'

'It does. It is. Or rather it was.' Rafe lay back in his chair regarding the other man through narrowed eyes. 'So what do you want me to say? That I have got more money than sense?'

'That would be a start.'

Steve grimaced and then, meeting Rafe's gaze, he moved his shoulders in a defensive gesture. 'Hey, it's your decision. I'm only an employee.' He paused. 'It wouldn't have anything to do with a certain Ms Fielding, would it? You're not bailing Myers out to help her?'

'No.'

Rafe's response was crisp and sharp and he swung forward in his chair, signalling the end of that discussion. He took a deep breath, calming himself.

'As a matter of fact, I am thinking of taking a trip. It is a while since I visited Miami. *Mi padre*— my father—he is of the opinion that I have forgotten all about him.'

Steve frowned. 'You could always invite your father to come here for a visit.'

'While there is a chance that Sarah might turn up and create havoc?' suggested Rafe drily. 'I do not think so. In any case, I will enjoy a change of scene.'

And what an understatement that was, he thought

broodingly. Since being with Lily, he hadn't been able to concentrate on anything else.

Also, he didn't like the fact that Steve had seen through his reasons for investing in Cartagena Charters so easily. Lily probably wouldn't welcome his involvement in the company either.

Yet, despite all the promises he'd made to himself when he'd left the rectory, he was still infatuated with her. However pathetic it was, this would give him a legitimate excuse for seeing her again.

'You don't fancy flying up to Newport to bring the yacht back to the island?' Steve suggested hopefully, but Rafe shook his head.

'If you want the yacht, you go and fetch it,' remarked Rafe carelessly, and wasn't totally surprised when Steve objected.

'And leave you here on your own with that psycho on the loose?' he exclaimed. 'Not gonna happen.'

Rafe sighed. 'So, okay. We will go to Miami instead.' He shuffled the papers in front of him. 'We will leave at the end of the week.'

'Okay.' Steve was forced to give in. 'But you be careful until we leave, right? I'm still not convinced I was mistaken about you-know-who.'

'Nor am I.' Rafe sighed. 'But you did check that no one of that name had arrived on the island.'

'Like she's gonna use her own name,' retorted Steve drily. 'Come on, she's not that dumb.'

'No.' Rafe shook his head. 'You could be right.'

'So don't go out alone again,' said Steve severely. 'Humour me until we're sure she's not here.'

It was lunchtime again and Lily was alone in the agency. Ray had left about five minutes ago to make his regular trip to the bar, and Lily was using the time to sort out the contents of his desk.

Along with candy wrappers and empty fast food cartons, the drawers were filled with unpaid bills and old bank statements, none of which made very happy reading.

Still, she thought, once Rafe's accountants took a hand she wouldn't have to worry about angry debtors storming in the door.

And all the charter craft would as like as not get a thorough overhaul. She doubted the Oliveira Corporation would risk its reputation by not doing its homework.

She heard the outer door open and close and frowned in annoyance. Wasn't it just like Ray to come back early when she was riffling through his desk? But so what? she thought impatiently. She'd rather that Rafe's money men didn't think that she didn't know how to do her job.

Footsteps approached the screen, lighter footsteps than Ray's, and Lily looked up in surprise. A woman was standing in the opening that separated the two parts of the agency. A tall attractive woman with blonde hair and unusually intense blue eyes.

She was wearing a cream slip dress, which clung

to her generous curves, and perilously high heels. A beige clutch bag was tucked beneath her arm. An unusual outfit, Lily thought, for someone who apparently wanted to charter a yacht. The customers she was used to dealing with wore shorts, or jeans and deck shoes.

'Hi,' Lily said, closing the drawer and getting up from Ray's desk and coming towards her. 'Can I help you?'

A smile played about the woman's lips. 'I hope so,' she said, and Lily was aware that she was giving her a thorough once-over.

Well, okay, she thought. In a navy patterned shirt, tied at the waist, and shorts, she didn't look much like your typical office worker. But she was efficient. As this woman would find out if she'd tell her what she had in mind.

'Are you looking for a charter?' she asked politely, ignoring the appraisal, and the woman cupped one elbow in her free hand and allowed her fingers to play against her lips.

'I may be,' she said at last. She gestured behind her. 'Those boats in the slips: do they all belong to the agency?'

'Um...some of them,' said Lily, not wanting to admit how many of their craft were idle at this time. 'How big a boat were you interested in hiring?'

The woman's brows drew together. 'I'm not sure,' she said, after a moment. 'Perhaps you could show me what you have?'

'Oh, well...' Lily hesitated. 'As a matter of fact, I don't handle that side of the business. Mr Myers does.'

'But Mr Myers is not here,' said the woman pointedly. She glanced all about her. 'Unless he is hiding in the filing cabinet.' Her eyes returned to Lily's. 'Are you saying you can't deal with me yourself?'

Lily pursed her lips. Wasn't this just typical? she thought. A whole morning without a customer and just when Ray was absent a possible client turned up.

Of course she could turn the woman away. She could make the excuse—which Ray himself had made many times in the past—that he didn't like to close the agency, even over a lunchtime.

But she was very much afraid that if she did, the woman would find an alternative agency. And, at the present time, any customer was welcome.

'I suppose I could show you what we have,' she said at last, shoving her own bag into the cupboard below her desk and picking up Ray's keys. 'But I can't close the agency for long.'

'No problem,' said the woman, who had a distinctly North American accent. 'I'm Sally Frances, by the way. And you're—?'

'Lily. Lily Fielding,' she said quickly but, as the woman moved back to allow her to pass into the front of the agency, she felt a sudden sense of unease.

There was something wrong here, she thought. The woman didn't look like a customer. She didn't even act like any customer Lily had dealt with. She

apparently didn't know how big a boat she was looking for or say how many people it was to accommodate.

She was polite and well-dressed, yet there was
something odd about her. And those eyes! Lily shivered. They wore an expression she'd never seen before.

They stepped out onto the street and Lily locked
the door behind them. Then she looked about her.
There was no sign of Ray, but that wasn't unexpected.

Nevertheless, she was tempted to excuse herself
and run to the bar and fetch him. Or leave him a note,
telling him where she'd gone.

Only her pride kept her from doing either of those
things. She'd had enough criticism in the past few
days. And heavens, she assured herself, what did she
think the woman was going to do? It was broad daylight. There were plenty of people about.

But there weren't plenty of people about when
they entered the marina. The yachts that weren't on
charter were just rocking at their moorings, and the
chief sounds were of fenders bumping against the
jetty and the sucking of the water around the hulls.
Even the repair sheds were deserted, most of the men
taking a liquid lunch.

Realising the woman was waiting for her to
extol the virtues of the various types of vessel, Lily
glanced back over her shoulder. And was reassured
when she saw that Sally Frances was struggling to

avoid her heels from slipping between the wooden slats of the pier.

It made the fact that she was between Lily and the exit seem less daunting. Lily was fairly sure that if the woman tried anything she could push her into the harbour.

Which was a ridiculous thought to have. Dismissing it, she pointed to the first yacht that belonged to the agency. It was a fairly new ketch, with aluminium masts and twin diesel engines. Hoping she sounded more knowledgeable than she felt, she said, 'This one sleeps six and does an average of fourteen knots.'

That strange smile tugged at the woman's mouth again. 'Let's go a little further,' she said, moving forward, forcing Lily to back along the gangway. 'What are these yachts doing? Are they all waiting to be chartered?'

'Some,' said Lily vaguely, still hedging. 'If I knew what you were looking for—'

'I'll know it when I see it,' said Sally Frances lightly. 'Let's see: how about that one?'

She was pointing to the boat that they'd had such a problem with. The *Santa Lucia* had limped back from Jamaica the previous day and for once Ray had taken his engineer's advice and booked it in for a complete overhaul.

'Oh, I'm sorry—' Lily began, turning back to explain that that particular yacht was out of service. 'If you could choose another...'

'I want to see this boat,' the woman said, indicating that she wanted to get on board. 'Or do you want me to tell your employer that you refused my request?'

Lily was tempted to say she didn't care what Sally Frances told her employer. But the thought of how stupid it would make her look if she told Ray she'd been nervous about getting on the boat with the woman because she was on her own made her lift her shoulders in defeat.

'Okay,' she said, grasping the mooring line to steady herself as she stepped on board.

She turned to offer Sally Frances her hand, but the woman had kicked off her high heels and jumped agilely over the gunwale to land on the deck beside her.

Too close, thought Lily, swallowing convulsively. Would anyone hear her if she cried for help?

Unfortunately, the slips seemed deserted. It was lunchtime, as she'd acknowledged earlier, and not a particularly busy time of year. Besides, she was worrying unnecessarily. What on earth did she expect the woman to do?

'I'd like to see the cabin.'

The woman had followed her as she'd tried to put some space between them. Without her high heels, Sally Frances had no trouble keeping her balance as she'd done before.

The momentary hope Lily had had that she'd left her shoes on the pier was dashed when she saw the woman was carrying them. Without leaving any word for Ray, there was nothing to indicate where they were.

'What are we waiting for?'

The woman was getting impatient and, unless she refused to go down into the cabin, Lily knew there was nothing she could do. This wasn't a situation she'd ever had to deal with before—thank God! And, although she was sure she ought to make an effort to deal with the woman more firmly, something about her put Lily on edge.

What would her father do? she wondered, as she descended the steps into the main saloon. Pray for guidance, she guessed, only in her case her mind was blank.

She wished Dee-Dee was here. For the first time in her life, she wished she'd taken more notice of the West Indian woman when she'd tried to persuade her to attend one of her ceremonies.

Was it possible to influence someone by getting inside their mind?

Something told her that whatever she did, Sally Frances was unlikely to be impressed.

Concentrating hard, Lily brought Dee-Dee's face into her mind. She'd never tried to communicate with the West Indian woman in this way before, but there was always a first time. Her father might not believe in ESP, but Lily had seen enough to know that it was a reality.

But, unfortunately, it seemed, Dee-Dee had powers she didn't have.

As she'd anticipated, nothing happened. It would have been a miracle indeed if it had, she thought ruefully. Instead, she put the width of the cabin between her and her visitor. If Dee-Dee couldn't help her, she would have to help herself.

She found herself thinking about Rafe. It was ironic that he should come to the forefront of her thoughts at this time. She wondered where he was, what he was doing. Would he ever forgive her for accusing him of having an affair with Laura Mathews? Or of wanting to get back with his ex-wife?

Meanwhile, the woman was getting impatient. Gesturing towards one of the banquettes, she said, 'Why don't we sit down? It's so much easier to talk if we're relaxed.'

Relaxed!

Lily felt a spurt of hysteria rising in her throat at the idea that she might ever feel relaxed with this woman. But she had to remain calm and, because her legs weren't entirely steady, she subsided onto one of the cushioned seats with some relief.

'Now, Ms Fielding…'

To her surprise, Sally Frances didn't sit down, but opened the bag she'd had tucked under her arm instead. Lily stiffened, half afraid the woman was going to produce a gun. But that was ridiculous, she told herself, only to jump back when Sally Frances tossed a cell phone onto the seat beside her.

'I want you to make a call for me.'

'A call?' Lily was confused. 'What do you mean?'

'You know how to use a cell phone, don't you?'

'Well...yes.'

'Okay. I want you to make a call.' The woman leaned back against the polished wood behind her. 'Don't look so surprised...um... Lily, isn't it? Did you honestly think I'd hire a boat from you?'

Lily blinked, trying not to look as anxious as she felt. 'Then what are we doing here?'

'You'll find out.' The woman bent and put on her shoes again. 'I assume you've guessed the number I want you to call.'

'No!' Lily stared at her in confusion. But when she tried to get to her feet the woman left her stance and moved intimidatingly towards her.

'Stay where you are,' she said. 'I don't want to hurt you. But I'm bigger than you are and I'm quite an expert in martial arts.'

'But who am I to call?' Lily asked again, her throat dry. 'I don't have any money, and if you're thinking of blackmailing Ray—'

'Be quiet!' The woman spoke coldly. 'I know all about the agency: who owns it, what you do there, where you live. I've had someone watching you for days, *Ms* Fielding. I know everything there is to know about you.'

Lily swallowed. 'Why would anything I do interest you?'

She blinked rapidly, suddenly remembering the man who they'd thought had been following Rafe. Perhaps he'd been following her instead.

And that night on the beach when she'd gone swimming...

She shivered, recalling her apprehension.

But why?

Then another thought occurred to her.

'If you're from the United States government, I can tell you I've never been involved with drugs in my life!'

'I believe you.' The woman was sardonic.

'Then—?'

The woman suddenly lost patience with the delay. 'Pick up the phone,' she ordered grimly. 'I won't ask you again.'

Lily reached for the cell phone with hands that were damp with perspiration. She was sweating freely and the slim cylinder slid uselessly from her grasp.

It landed at Sally's feet. And for a brief moment Lily speculated whether she could pretend to stumble as she reached for it and knock the other woman's legs from under her.

But, even as she considered this, Sally kicked the phone away.

'Don't even think of it,' she said contemptuously. 'You may be expendable, Ms Fielding, but not until you've made the call to Rafe.' She paused. 'Now, pick up the phone. And if you insist you don't know what number to call, I'll tell you.'

CHAPTER FIFTEEN

RAFE WAS STARING unseeingly out of his study windows when the phone rang.

He waited for a moment, expecting his PA to answer it, and then remembered he didn't have a PA. He wasn't living in New York anymore. He was here, in Orchid Cay, wondering how the hell he was going to live without Lily in his life.

Reaching for the receiver, he glanced automatically at the caller's identity. But the screen showed only the word 'Unknown' and he felt an uneasy prickling at the back of his neck.

He was tempted not to answer it, the image of his ex-wife flashing briefly into his mind. But then, with an exclamation, he reached for the receiver. If it was Sarah, she'd get bloody short shrift from him.

'Sí?' he said crisply, not identifying himself or his number, and heard the caller take an unsteady breath before replying.

'Mr Oliveira?'

The female voice was unfamiliar to him. Not

Sarah then, he thought, not sure whether he was relieved or sorry. Until he knew exactly where his ex-
wife was and what she was doing, he would always
have this feeling of unease.

'Yes,' he said shortly. 'Who is this?'

'My name is Dee-Dee Boudreaux, Mr Oliveira,'
said the woman at once. 'I work for the Reverend
Fielding, at the rectory.'

'*Sí*, I know who you are.'

Rafe knew his voice was becoming more clipped
by the minute, but he couldn't help it. Why was
someone who worked for the Fieldings calling him?

Unless... He swallowed. Unless something had
happened to either Lily or her father. Once again, he
thought of Sarah. But he still had no proof that she
was on the island.

Dee-Dee didn't seem to notice his abruptness. But
she was nervous. He could tell. 'Um...sorry to trouble you, Mr Oliveira, but...well, is Lily with you?'

'Lily?' His worst fears were realised.

'Lily Fielding,' agreed Dee-Dee. 'You remember
her, don't you, Mr Oliveira?'

Rafe swore. 'Of course I remember her!' he exclaimed harshly. How could he forget? 'What is this
all about?'

'Well, is she with you or not?'

'No, she is not with me.' Rafe curbed another
oath. 'Why would you think she was?' He paused.
'Did she tell you she was coming to Orchid Point?
Because, if so, she has not arrived.'

And that was disturbing in itself.

Dee-Dee sounded agitated now. 'So where is she?' she muttered, but Rafe had the feeling she was talking as much to herself as to him. 'She's not answering her phone or the phone at the agency. No one is. And that's odd, 'cos she always told me that man, Myers, he don't like closing in the middle of the day.'

'Wait—' Rafe broke in, his own nerves jangling now '—let me get this straight. You have been trying to reach Lily on both her own phone and the phone at the agency and she is not answering either, *sí*?'

'Yessir.'

'Well—' Rafe could feel a headache coming on, and the pulse in his temple was throbbing painfully. 'She could be anywhere, could she not? Does she not sometimes have a picnic lunch in…in Palmetto Park?'

And why had he thought of that?

'She always has her phone with her, Mr Oliveira. She keeps it in her bag.' Dee-Dee groaned, muttering to herself under her breath. 'I got this feeling, see, Mr Oliveira? Like she was trying to tell me she was in danger.'

'And you immediately thought of me?' Rafe's tone was bitter. '*Bien*, it is good to know you have such a high opinion of my character.'

'I didn't know what to think,' retorted Dee-Dee defensively. 'I get these messages sometimes and I don't always know where they're from.'

'Messages?'

Rafe must have sounded incredulous because Dee-Dee clicked her tongue. 'I knew you wouldn't believe me. But I don't care what you think, Mr Oliveira. I'm sure Lily's in danger. And, whatever you say, the feeling ain't going away.'

Rafe sucked in a breath. He didn't have a reason for doing so, but he believed her. After all, he'd lived much of his childhood amongst people to whom black magic was a way of life.

*Macumba, voodoo, juju...*whatever name it went by, he respected its power. And he also knew that not all experiences could be explained away by logic.

'Okay,' he said, and he could tell by her sudden expulsion of breath that she'd sensed his capitulation. 'What do you want me to do?'

'Could you go to the agency?' asked Dee-Dee at once. 'Find that man she works for and ask him where she is. Believe me, Mr Oliveira, I wouldn't be asking you to get involved unless I was certain something bad is going down.'

'And have you spoken to her father?'

'No!' Dee-Dee was scornful now. 'I love that man, Mr Oliveira, but he won't listen to me. If I tell him I got one of my feelings, he'll tell me to go and pray for forgiveness, you know what I mean?'

Rafe did know. Much as he respected Lily's father, he could well believe that William Fielding closed his eyes to anything he didn't want to see. Or hear.

'Bien,' he said, pushing back his chair. 'I will go

to the agency. Give me your number and if I find her I will let you know.'

'You're a good man, Mr Oliveira. I don't care what anyone says.' Dee-Dee was passionately grateful. 'I'm afraid, wherever Lily is, she's in a whole heap of trouble!'

Rafe left Orchid Point ten minutes later.

He was alone because, although he'd tried to get in touch with Steve, he wasn't answering his phone.

Rafe had sent the other man to the airport, to check out the Cessna for their flight to Miami the following day. He guessed Steve had turned his phone off before he entered the airport buildings.

It was a little after two o'clock when he got to the small town of Orchid Cay. Parking the car in a no-waiting area across from the agency, he strode over the road and into the building.

So someone must be here, he thought, acknowledging the unlocked door. He hoped it was Lily. It would be worth the drive just to reassure himself that she was safe.

There was no one behind the counter so he wasted no time in rounding the partition into the back office. But its only occupant was Myers, seated at his desk, his scowl directed towards the visitor.

'Where the hell have you be—?'

He broke off abruptly when he saw Rafe, but it was obvious what he'd been about to say. Myers hadn't seen Lily either and the ominous feeling in Rafe's stomach kicked up another notch.

'Oh—sorry, Mr Oliveira.' Myers got hurriedly to his feet, colouring with embarrassment. 'I thought you were my assistant. Lily hasn't shown her face since lunchtime and I'm just about at the end of my patience.'

'Really?'

Rafe's response was bland, but he found he needed a moment to absorb the situation. Lily wasn't here. That was obvious. And, from the expression on Myers' face, he thought Rafe agreed with him.

'Yes, really,' he said vigorously. 'And this isn't the first time she's taken off without my permission. It's not good enough, Mr Oliveira. I'm her employer, for God's sake. I expect some loyalty from my staff.'

Rafe's head was throbbing now and, although he would have liked to expunge some of his frustration by giving this cocky little man the hiding he felt he deserved, he restrained himself. Instead, he said, 'If you mean the other day, she was with me.' He paused, endeavouring to calm himself. 'So, where is she now? Have you tried to find her?'

'To find her?' Ray blinked. 'No.' He broke off and then continued defiantly, 'I assumed she was with you, actually. I'm not a complete fool, Mr Oliveira. I know what's going on.'

'Do you?' Rafe's tone was menacing. 'Well, we will not go into what you mean by that right now.

Where do you think she might be, Myers? And, I warn you, do not try to be clever with me.'

Ray's face grew sulky. 'It's not my place to go looking for her,' he muttered. 'Maybe she's showing someone round the marina. The door was locked when I got here. It was lucky I had a spare set of keys.' He snorted. 'Maybe she's got some other mug on the side.'

'And maybe you would like to take a swim in the harbour,' said Rafe savagely, somewhat mollified when the other man looked alarmed.

Swearing, he strode across the office, aware that Myers cowered away from him as he did so. 'Have you checked to see if she has left any message about where she might have gone?'

'No.' Ray was distinctly unhappy now. 'Look, it's not my fault if she's not here. I'm the one who should be angry, not you. She'll come back when she's ready and not before.'

'*Imbecil!*' Rafe riffled through the papers lying beside Lily's computer and then, finding nothing, he pulled open the cupboard below the desk. '*Mierda!*' he exclaimed, finding Lily's bag and holding it up for Ray to see. 'Does she usually go for lunch without her handbag?'

Ray was still searching for something to say when Rafe's phone rang. Pulling the cell out of his pocket, he checked the identity of his caller and was reassured when he saw it was Steve.

'You got my message,' he said at once, without

giving the other man time to speak. 'Good. We've got a problem.'

'Haven't we just?' Steve's response was totally unexpected. 'Where are you?'

'I'm at the Cartagena agency,' said Rafe. 'Where are you?'

'I'm on my way into town,' said Steve grimly. 'Stay where you are till I arrive.'

He paused and then added reluctantly, 'Sarah's got Lily. She had her ring the house to speak to you, but you weren't there. Luckily I was, so I took the call. Apparently, Sarah knows about you two, and she's not happy.'

Lily knew the call she'd made to Orchid Point had angered the woman. She'd been infuriated to hear that Rafe wasn't there. Lily had tried to tell her it wouldn't have meant anything anyway, that she meant nothing to Rafe, but obviously the woman didn't believe her.

The woman still hadn't told her who she was, although Lily had guessed. Her references to Rafe, the fury she'd shown when he hadn't been available to answer the call, had proved her identity.

Besides, she still wore a wedding ring and a huge ruby on her third finger. Who else could she be but Rafe's ex-wife?

Yet what could she possibly hope to gain by kidnapping her? Lily wondered uneasily. Didn't the woman know he'd gone looking for her a few days ago? It couldn't be because she believed Rafe cared about Lily. That was nonsense. Rafe had made his feelings about her very plain by staying away.

But perhaps she didn't know that. And would she believe it if Lily tried to tell her?

'*Jesus!*' the woman swore angrily. Since Lily had ended the call she'd been striding restlessly about the cabin. Lily wondered if it was done to calm her nerves. Or perhaps she was hoping to frighten her companion.

She was certainly making Lily nervous. The thought had crossed her mind that maybe Sally intended to knock her out and dump her body in the harbour. With the water in the marina probably polluted with diesel oil, she wouldn't give much for her chances if that was so.

But to imagine Mrs Oliveira as a murderess was pushing the bounds of belief. Or so Lily told herself.

'We can't waste any more time.'

Lily's mouth dried. What now? After forcing her to make that phone call, Lily had few doubts left about the woman's balance of mind.

She'd told Lily to tell Rafe—or, as he wasn't there, his assistant—that she had his girlfriend. That he'd better get himself down to the marina post-haste or she wouldn't be responsible for the consequences.

Watching the woman circling the cabin, Lily tried to calculate how much time she'd have if she attempted to escape. She could make her bid when the woman was furthest away from the companionway. She might have five seconds to reach the stairs. Would that be enough?

And what did she have to lose?

'Okay, we're going back on deck,' said the woman abruptly, and Lily blinked in surprise.

Plan B, she thought, wondering if this might work for her too. On deck, she might have a chance of attracting someone's attention. Or had the woman decided she couldn't wait any longer to exact whatever revenge she planned to take?

Lily got up from the banquette on legs that felt decidedly unsteady. She doubted now that she could have raced up the steps if she'd had the chance. They were steep and possibly slippery and her hands were sweating. She would have been more likely to slip and break her neck.

Which might have saved Sally a job.

Then another thought occurred to her: if the woman was behind her, could she kick out and maybe knock her back into the cabin? All she needed was a bit of luck. Then she could run like crazy back to the quay.

But, predictably, Sally had thought of that too. 'Don't go getting any ideas,' she said, taking hold of one of Lily's arms and twisting it up behind her back. 'If you make one wrong move, I'll break this.'

Lily believed her as she grasped the handrail with her sweat-slick fingers. 'Why should I care?' she demanded, refusing to let the woman see her panic. 'I've got nothing to lose.'

'Good point.' Sally gave a short mirthless laugh. 'You're not as stupid as you look. Which makes a change. Rafe's women are usually thick as planks.'

Lily's stomach tightened. Despite her earlier doubts about him, subsequent events made her think Rafe wasn't a womaniser. But she was very much afraid it wasn't going to matter either way.

It was slightly cooler on deck but, although Lily looked helplessly about her, there was no one in sight. Dear God, she thought grimly, where was Ray Myers when she needed him? It was after two o'clock. Lunchtime was over. He would normally have been on her case.

'Over there.' Sally gestured towards the wheelhouse. 'You do know how to start the engines, don't you?'

Lily stared at her blankly. Her idea of what was going to happen next needed serious revision. What on earth was the woman planning? Why, in God's name, did she want her to start the engines?

'You do know how to start the bloody thing, don't you?'

Sally was impatient, and Lily tried to think what she should do. Yes, she knew the principles of starting the powerful motors. But was that enough?

And this was the *Santa Lucia*, she reminded herself. Its engines were old and they were already desperate for repair. According to Dave Tapply, it was a miracle that either they, or the group who'd hired the craft, had made it back to Orchid Cay in one piece.

When you were dealing with petroleum, there was always the danger that it could cause a fire.

She thought about telling Sally that and swiftly abandoned the idea. The woman was never going to believe her. There was so much bitterness in her face, Lily found herself wishing the engines would start. Surely Sally would let her go once they were out of the harbour?

Or not.

But she didn't want to think that far ahead.

Hoping against hope that someone might see them, Lily allowed herself to be propelled towards the console. The arm Sally was pushing was painful, but a broken arm seemed less important now.

The keys were in the ignition. No one in their right mind would try to steal the *Lucia*, she thought resignedly. Everyone who used the marina knew that the boat wasn't seaworthy.

With a brief glance at the woman beside her, she used her free hand to turn the key and press the ignition.

Nothing happened at first. An ominous silence seemed to have fallen over the marina.

But when she pressed again there was a low rumble from below deck. Like a car's engine whose carburettor had been flooded, the engines turned over. But they didn't start. No matter how often she tried, the result was always the same.

Aware that Sally was close behind her, Lily renewed her efforts. But it was a distinctly weaker sound now. As Dave had said, it was a miracle that either of the engines had fired, and now it seemed they'd both given up the ghost.

'Why isn't it starting?'

Getting angry, the woman forced Lily to move aside and reached for the ignition. She pressed the button herself, over and over again. But the only re-action she got was the groan of protesting machinery.

'What the hell's the matter with it?' she demanded. 'Is it out of gas?'

Lily, who'd been jammed against the console, tried to humour her. 'It—it might be,' she said, glancing about her. 'Do you want me to see if I can find a spare can—?'

She broke off abruptly. Although she knew she must be imagining things, she could have sworn she'd seen someone on the deck of the boat that was moored alongside the *Lucia*.

A shadow had moved and then concealed itself behind the wheelhouse. Dear God, it had looked a lot like Rafe. Which only showed how desperate she'd become.

'Do I want you to see if you can find a spare what?'

Sally was waiting for her answer, and Lily struggled to remember what she'd said.

'A…a spare can of gas,' she stammered, forcing herself not to look towards the other vessel. 'There might be one stored…stored below.'

'Yeah, right.' Sally forced Lily's arm further up

her back until she had to bite her tongue to stop herself from crying out in agony. 'Do you honestly think I'm going to let you go rummaging about down there on your own?' She swore. 'How the hell am I going to get this heap out of the harbour? Dammit, it must work. It got here, didn't it?'

For a moment, her attention was diverted by the need to start the engines, and Lily attempted to ease the hold on her arm. But Sally didn't let go and the pain became excruciating. 'You're wasting your time,' she told her contemptuously. 'Forget it, little girl. You're not leaving. If Rafe doesn't come, you'll have to take the consequences instead.'

She pressed the ignition once more and, as she did so, Lily took the chance to glance towards the other boat again.

With a mixture of relief and dismay, she saw Rafe wedged between the cabin and the rail. She hadn't been mistaken. He was just a few yards away.

Rafe saw her too, but he shook his head to deter her from reacting. Not that she needed his warning. She had no intention of drawing the other woman's attention to him.

Nevertheless, guessing he was going to try and board the *Lucia*, Lily felt her heart accelerate. Did he know how unpredictable, not to say dangerous, his ex-wife was? If she thought Rafe had come to Lily's rescue, God knew how she'd take her revenge.

'Do you think it could be the key?' she offered

hurriedly now, desperate to distract the woman's attention, and Sally gave her another scornful look.

'Don't be stupid!' she exclaimed. 'The engines wouldn't have turned over at all if that were true.' She kicked the base of the unit, her temper growing. 'Dammit, it's got to start.'

But, although she tried again, nothing happened and, with a sudden burst of fury, she slammed her fist down onto the console, causing the boat to rock at its moorings.

And, as she did so, a screwdriver that had been lying on the console tumbled to the floor.

It was a big screwdriver, long and heavy, and Lily guessed it had been used by one of the engineers checking out the faulty engines. If she could just get hold of it...

She caught her breath. Sally didn't appear to have noticed what had happened. She was too intent on jamming her finger on the ignition over and over again. What she hoped to achieve, Lily couldn't imagine. It was obvious the engines weren't going to turn over again.

Lily clenched her teeth. If she could just get free she could use the screwdriver to defend herself. And Rafe, she thought determinedly. She doubted he had brought a weapon with him.

She hadn't the first idea where he was at this particular moment. She daren't look at the other vessel in case she drew attention to herself. If Sally guessed her ex-husband was in the vicinity, God alone knew how she might react.

Lily's arm was throbbing, but that was the least of her worries. She had to get away from Sally. She had to do something to save herself before Rafe came charging to the rescue.

Then there was a sound like the roar of an approaching train. The boat bucked savagely beneath them and Sally was obliged to release Lily to save herself. And, despite the agony in her arm, Lily lunged wildly for the screwdriver that had rolled to within an inch of falling into the dock.

She almost lost her balance, and she wondered if Rafe was responsible for what was happening. But then there was another almighty blast, and she was thrown violently off her feet.

The screwdriver went flying, and she felt the deck come up to meet her. She landed hard, unable to suppress a groan when her injured arm hit the floor.

She rolled towards the rail, trying to put some distance between her and her tormentor, but the pain in her arm had made her sick. Where was Rafe? she wondered dizzily. Where was Sally? Then something solid hit her on the back of her head and she knew no more...

CHAPTER SIXTEEN

SHE WAS AWAKENED by a man in a white coat leaning over her, directing the light from a torch onto her aching pupils. The light was white, vividly white, as was the room in which she was lying. She was in a strange white world and she heard herself give a moan of protest.

Then two things happened simultaneously. The man's face broke into a smile of satisfaction and Rafe appeared at the man's shoulder, almost elbowing him aside to get close to her.

'*Querida,*' he said, lifting her limp hand from the coverlet, and she was almost sure his voice shook a little as he spoke. He raised her hand to his lips, the relief on his face plain to see. '*Dios, querida*, we have been so worried about you.'

'Mr Oliveira.' The man who Lily now realised must be a doctor spoke mildly, but it was obvious that he expected to be obeyed. 'I understand your concern, particularly in the circumstances, but you must allow me to finish my examination of Ms Fielding.'

Rafe released her hand with evident reluctance and stepped back from the bed. At the same time, her father moved into her line of vision, his studious face showing the same strain Rafe's had exhibited.

Lily tried to smile at him, wanting to show him he didn't have to worry. But then, as the doctor was examining her head, running exploratory fingers over her scalp, he touched a sensitive spot at the back of her skull and she nearly jumped out of her skin.

'Ah,' he said consideringly, as both Rafe and her father offered a protest. 'That is tender, is it not? And no wonder. Something hit your head with considerable force.'

Lily drew a trembling breath. Until that moment her reasons for being in what was apparently a hospital bed had been shadowy, vague, existing somewhere just beyond the reach of her conscious mind.

But the doctor's words had torn the veil aside.

'I—Rafe—' she began, looking beseechingly towards him and, once again, he came swiftly to her side.

'Just rest, *querida*,' he said. 'Permit the doctor to complete his examination. We will talk, I promise you. When you are feeling stronger.'

'But, Rafe—your wife—'

'Lily...' Rafe looked helplessly at the doctor and, with a gesture of assent, the man nodded his head. 'Lily, Sarah was badly injured in the accident. I will tell you all about it later.'

Lily stared at him. 'What happened?' she asked anxiously. 'Were you hurt too?'

'Later,' the doctor intervened. 'You know, you have been very lucky. That blow you suffered could have killed you.'

Lily gazed at him weakly, the throbbing in her head making every movement an agony. 'Then what—?'

'A little concussion is all,' declared the doctor, straightening to address his remarks to Rafe and her father. 'A few days' rest and recuperation and she should be as good as new.'

'Thank God!' Her father spoke for the first time, coming to stand beside the bed, gazing down at her with anxious eyes. 'When Mr Oliveira told me what had happened, I was devastated. You could have been killed, as Dr Martinez says, and what would I have done then?'

Lily managed a weak smile. It was typical of her father to think of himself first.

'Well, I'm still here,' she said huskily, allowing him to take her hand. 'I'm all right, really. I've just got a bad headache, that's all.'

'I can give you something for that,' said the doctor, and William Fielding moved aside.

'I want your assurance that my daughter will receive the best of care while she's in the hospital, Dr Martinez,' he said stiffly. 'She's very precious to me. Whatever it costs, we'll find the money somehow.'

Lily groaned. 'Daddy—'

'Oh, but there is no need for Ms Fielding to stay in the hospital,' protested Dr Martinez at once. 'We'll keep her overnight, of course, just to ensure there are no other surprises. Tomorrow she can return home. She must rest, you understand, and I would recommend a light diet for the next few days. But time is a great healer. She should make a full recovery.'

He smiled at both men before returning his attention to Lily's father. 'Mr Fielding, we find patients recover much more quickly in their own homes.'

'It's Reverend Fielding, actually,' said William Fielding in his usual pedantic way. 'But I'm not at all sure that sending Lily home is such a good idea. I'm a busy man, Martinez. Who is going to look after her? I love my daughter dearly, but I am no good in the sickroom.'

'Daddy—' Lily tried to speak, but Rafe forestalled her.

'Do not concern yourself, Reverend,' he said, his eyes darkening as they rested on Lily's pale face. 'With your permission, I will arrange for Lily to stay at Orchid Point for the period of her convalescence. I will see that a nurse is employed and, rest assured, she will receive the best of care.'

William Fielding was obviously taken aback, and Lily waited for him to say that of course that wouldn't be necessary, that somehow he and Dee-Dee would manage.

But he didn't say anything of the kind. When he spoke again, it was to thank Rafe for his offer. 'That might be best,' he said with evident relief. 'I'm sure Lily joins me in appreciating your kindness.'

'Daddy!'

Lily stared disbelievingly at her father. She was fairly sure that Rafe was just being polite, that he felt some kind of responsibility for what had happened. But she didn't want to be beholden to him if that was all it was.

'Now, Lily—' began her father in that condescending tone he used sometimes, as Lily attempted to lever herself up from the pillow.

'Daddy, you can't—' she got out before the pain in her head stifled her protest. Groaning, she sank back against the pillows, and this time Rafe brooked no interference as he bent and touched her face with his hand.

'Let me,' he said huskily, his eyes dark and disturbingly possessive. 'Let me look after you, *querida*. I need... I need to be able to look after you. Humour me, Lily. I am in torment. These last few days have been the worst of my life!'

Lily swallowed, the pain subsiding as she relaxed again. 'There's no need,' she whispered softly, but Rafe merely bent and brushed his lips against her cheek.

'There is every need,' he told her thickly. 'I have gone through hell since I got word of your phone call. The way I feel at present, I never want to let you out of my sight again.'

* * *

It was not until two days later that Lily found out what had happened after she'd lost consciousness on the *Santa Lucia*.

With William Fielding's blessing, Rafe had arranged for an ambulance to transport her from the hospital in town to his house at Orchid Point the following day.

There, a uniformed nurse who had accompanied her from the hospital supervised her installation in a guest suite off the galleried landing. Then settled her to rest between cool linen sheets in a darkened room.

Rafe kept out of the way and Lily couldn't help wondering if he was regretting his generosity. But even the short journey from town had exhausted her and she was too weak to worry about that now.

After the nurse had drawn the blinds, she left her. And Lily closed her eyes and fell instantly asleep.

She was unaware of it, but she slept for more than sixteen hours.

Rafe was concerned and was constantly checking on her, but the nurse, a young West Indian woman, assured him she'd come to no harm. She was keeping a close eye on her patient's condition, she told him. She would know immediately if anything was wrong.

Lily awoke early the following morning. The room was shadowy because the blinds were still drawn, but slatted rays of sunlight were making a pattern on the ceiling above her head.

She thought at first she was alone, but then she

saw Rafe, slouched in a chair by the windows. He appeared to be asleep, his head thrown back, his hands hanging loosely over the arms of the cushioned rocker.

She wondered how long he'd been there. Some time, she suspected, judging by the shadow of stubble on his jaw. She shifted on her pillows, dreading the blinding pain she'd suffered in recent days. But, apart from a twinge of discomfort, she felt much better. Evidently, as Dr Martinez had said, time was a great healer.

She must have made a sound because Rafe stirred at once. Pushing himself up almost before he was fully conscious, he stumbled unsteadily across the room.

'You are awake,' he said huskily, his eyes dark and searching. 'Do you know you have slept for hours?'

'Have I?' Lily was surprised. 'I must have been tired.'

'Tired, yes.' Rafe scrubbed the heel of his hand across his eyes and then stared blearily at his watch. 'How are you feeling?'

Lily blinked. 'I feel much better,' she said, aware that the throbbing in her head had almost gone. 'What time is it? It looks very bright outside.'

'It is a little after seven in the morning. A beautiful morning now that you are awake,' Rafe added fervently.

Lily stared at him. 'You mean I've slept almost a whole day?'

'Pretty much,' he agreed. 'But that is good. You

needed to rest.' He paused. 'So how does your head feel?'

'Better. Not so muzzy.' Lily moved against the pillows to show she could. 'The pain has virtually gone.'

'Gracias a Dios.' Rafe was pleased. 'Your father will be delighted. I have kept him informed of your progress. He has been very worried about you.'

Lily reserved judgement on that score. She shouldn't forget that her father was responsible for her being brought here in the first place.

Rafe nodded now. 'You must be hungry. I will get Carla to—'

Lily eased herself up against the pillows. 'Um... could I just have some water? I... I'm not hungry, but my mouth is...dry.'

'Por supuesto. Of course.' Rafe turned at once to the table beside the bed. Then he clicked his tongue. 'This water is warm. I will ask Carla to bring some fresh.'

'Warm is okay,' said Lily hurriedly. 'Honestly.'

Rafe's mouth twisted. 'If you are sure—?'

'I am.' Lily watched him pour some water from a tall jug into a glass, aware that the anticipation she was feeling wasn't only because she was thirsty. She couldn't help being aware of how completely alone they were in the bedroom.

And the vivid memories it evoked.

That awareness was heightened when Rafe bent to put his arm around her. 'Gently,' he said, bringing the glass to her lips. He muttered something to himself in Spanish and she could feel the tension emanating from him now. *'Dios,'* he added thickly, 'I do not know what I would have done if I had lost you, *querida.'*

It was hard to sip the warm liquid, knowing he was watching her so closely. She was so conscious of his nearness and, however welcome the water might have been, she couldn't ignore the intentness of his gaze.

What did it mean? What did he mean? She couldn't forget how she'd felt when she'd thought she was never going to see him again. She loved him, she thought incredulously. But how did he really feel about her?

'Thank you,' she managed at last, and he returned the glass to the bedside cabinet.

But, although he had no reason to allow his arm to remain about her shoulders, he didn't move away. Instead, he eased his hip onto the bed beside her, using his free hand to stroke her tumbled hair back from her forehead.

'Do you mind if I stay with you for a while?' he asked, and she realised his hand was trembling.

'I...no,' she replied a little breathlessly, and edged across the mattress to give him a little more room.

'But you do not want me to touch you, *no*?' he declared roughly, misunderstanding her actions. *'Bien.'* He got up from the bed. 'I do not blame you. Without me, you would not be in this position, would not have had to suffer the torment that my—*my*—ex-wife put you through.'

'Oh, Rafe.' Quite forgetting she was supposed to be an invalid, Lily pushed herself into a sitting position and, stretching out, grabbed his hand before he could move out of reach. 'Of course I don't mind if you touch me.' She shook her head impatiently. 'I don't blame you for any of this. It wasn't your fault that Sally—'

'Sarah,' he corrected her. 'That she went a little mad?' He completed the sentence for her. 'Perhaps it was. Perhaps I should never have married her.' He paused. 'But I did, and I should have realised before now that she was not totally sane, *no*?'

Lily gazed up at him helplessly. She became aware that she was wearing only a man-sized tee shirt and drew the sheet up to her chin. 'You didn't do anything wrong,' she insisted. 'It wasn't your fault that your marriage didn't work out.'

'You are very kind,' said Rafe gently, finding the sight of her in his floppy tee shirt more entrancing than she could ever know. The loose folds only hinted at the womanly shape beneath the fabric, but he remembered very well how beautiful she was.

'So tell me about—about Sarah,' she said. 'Where is she? Surely she hasn't been arrested.'

'Oh, no.' Rafe drew a long breath. 'Lily, Sarah is dead. She died in the explosion at the marina. It was a terrible tragedy, and my only consolation is that she must have known nothing about it.'

'Oh, my God!' Lily was horrified, and he realised she wasn't aware she'd clasped his hand to her breast. 'You mean the *Santa Lucia* blew up?' She shook her head. 'But how could that happen?'

'The engines exploded,' Rafe explained gently. He shrugged, overwhelmingly aware of the warmth of her breast against his hand. 'There is to be an investigation, of course, but it seems obvious from what your engineer—'

'Dave Tapply?'

'*Si*, from what he says, that one of the engines caught fire and he believes this caused the explosion.'

Lily could hardly take it all in. 'So how did I—?'

'Fortunately—and I do not use the term lightly— you were not next to Sarah when the explosion occurred. I believe you had lost your balance and rolled across the deck.'

Lily shivered. The screwdriver, she remembered grimly. Maybe groping for the screwdriver had saved her life.

'A spar of wood hit your head,' Rafe continued, unaware of what she was thinking. 'And, because you were near the rail, you were thrown into the water.'

CHAPTER SEVENTEEN

'I WAS THROWN into the water?' Lily could hardly believe it.

'*Sí*, and I was so afraid you would drown before I could reach you,' Rafe told her. 'The water was so cold.'

Lily stared at him. 'You pulled me out?' She vaguely remembered falling onto the deck, but nothing more.

'Somehow I got you both out,' he said, nodding. 'Regrettably, there was nothing I could do for Sarah. She was directly above the engines when the explosion occurred. It ripped the deck apart and she did not stand a chance.'

'Oh, Rafe!' Lily felt sick. 'I'm so sorry.'

'*Querida*, it was an accident. A terrible accident.' He paused. 'But can you ever forgive me?'

'Forgive you?' Lily was confused.

'For not realising that you might be in danger,' he told her huskily, his eyes dark with passion.

'You mustn't blame yourself.'

'But I do.' Rafe sighed. 'Steve had warned me that

Sarah was on the island. That was why—well, we do not have to go into that right now.' He paused. 'He was afraid she might try something. She had threatened me in the past, you see.'

'Oh, Rafe.'

She was beginning to understand why he had been so angry when she had accused him of going to meet his ex-wife. And she hadn't given him a proper chance to explain.

She sucked in a breath now as her brain struggled to absorb the situation. The memories his words had evoked caused her to shiver again.

'I tried to think of ways to get away from her,' she said unhappily. 'But she'd told me she was an expert in martial arts, and I knew I couldn't compete with that.'

'She wasn't an expert in anything,' said Rafe flatly, 'but you weren't to know that. I know from past experience what an accomplished liar she was.'

'She also said she'd had someone watching me. Do you think she saw me leaving your house?'

'Her detective might have done,' Rafe conceded. 'It was Sarah who hired the detective who was following us. Steve found this out. That was how he thought he had seen Sarah in the town.'

'And he had?'

'*Esta bien.*' Rafe nodded. 'Do you remember that afternoon you were at my house?'

Lily doubted she would ever forget, but she only nodded.

'When Steve came to the suite and woke me up to tell me this, I wanted to wake you. But you looked so peaceful lying there and I hoped to be back to explain. That was why when you awoke you were alone.'

Lily felt terrible. 'And, of course, I thought you'd gone to see another woman,' she remembered sadly.

'I had.' Rafe was sardonic. 'But not in the way you thought, *no*?'

'Oh, Rafe!'

'*Mierda*, do not look like that.' Rafe gazed at her ruefully. 'It was my job to protect you and I did a very poor job of it.'

Lily shrugged her slim shoulders. 'Well, it's over now. And, no matter what Sal—*Sarah*—was like, she didn't deserve to die.'

Rafe conceded the point. Then he added, 'Nor did you, *querida*. I would never have forgiven myself if anything bad had happened to you.'

Lily hesitated and then said softly, 'I thought you didn't want to see me again.'

'*Qué?*' Rafe was incredulous. 'How could you think that? I was the one who believed you did not wish to see me.'

'No!'

'But yes.' Rafe was determined. 'Do you not remember how angry you were because I left you without a word of explanation? I just threw on my clothes and drove into Orchid Cay.' He grimaced. 'I intended to tell you all about it when I got back but, as you know, you had left.'

Lily looked mortified and Rafe couldn't restrain the urge he had to touch her. His free hand curved around her chin, tipping her face up to his. Then, with the utmost tenderness, he kissed her lips, taking her swiftly expelled gulp of air into his mouth.

Then, returning to his explanation, he said, 'You can have no idea how I felt when I saw you on that boat, when I could see that Sarah was hurting you.' His voice was hoarse. 'Knowing how crazy she had become, I almost went out of my mind.'

'I was so afraid she would see you,' confessed Lily tremulously. 'I knew she hated me, but I think she hated you more.'

Rafe's lips tilted. 'You were afraid for me?' he ventured gently. 'That is good to know.'

'Well, of course I was,' Lily protested. 'I was trying to reach something to defend us both when there was this terrific noise and the boat seemed to rise out of the water.'

'You were searching for a weapon?' Rafe tried to distract her with his teasing comment. 'I had no idea you were so resourceful, Ms Fielding.'

'It was just a screwdriver,' said Lily defensively. 'I was trying to reach it when I rolled towards the rail.'

'How brave.' Rafe was no longer amused. He hesitated. 'So dare I think you care about me, after all?'

'Of course I care.' Lily's face took on a becoming colour. 'But you know that. Unlike you, I'm just an open book.'

'You think?' Rafe's eyes darkened. 'You certainly

wouldn't listen to my explanation when I came to the rectory that night.'

'I suppose I was suspicious of you.' Lily sighed. 'I'm sorry. But I still find it hard to believe that a man like you could be interested in a nobody like me.'

'Oh, Lily.' Rafe's hand left hers to probe beneath the hem of the tee shirt. His fingers found warm skin and the gentle mound of her stomach beneath the cotton fabric. His hand lingered momentarily over her navel, and then moved up to cup the fullness of her breast. 'You have no idea what you do to me.'

He paused and then, withdrawing his hand, he continued harshly, 'You know I am too old for you, do you not? I shall be forty on my next birthday, whereas you—you—'

'I'm twenty-four,' said Lily swiftly, capturing his hand and bringing it back to her breast. 'Does that really matter to you?'

'It should matter to you,' declared Rafe roughly. 'I know it will matter to your father, if I mention my intentions to him.'

'I don't care what my father thinks,' said Lily flatly. 'Well, of course I do, but he can't change my mind, if that's what you're afraid of.'

'Oh, *niña*.' Rafe shook his head expressively. 'You have come to mean so much to me. How can I ever let you go?'

'I hope you won't,' said Lily earnestly, and Rafe gave a rueful little laugh.

'And to think I might have been out of the country when all this happened.'

'Out of the country?' Lily stared at him. 'Were you planning on leaving Orchid Cay for good?'

'No.' Rafe shook his head. 'It was just a trip to Miami to see my father. It had crossed my mind that you might miss me while I was away.'

Lily expelled an unsteady breath. 'Thank goodness you didn't go.' She couldn't imagine what might have happened if Rafe hadn't been there to fish her out of the waters of the dock.

'Amen to that.' Rafe spoke fervently. '*Gracias a Dios* for Dee-Dee. If she hadn't got in touch with me—'

'Dee-Dee?' Lily's brows drew together. 'When did Dee-Dee get in touch with you?'

'About an hour before I found you. It was she who warned me you might be in danger.'

'But how did she know?'

Lily was incredulous, and Rafe went on to explain. 'She apparently had one of her "feelings",' he said, achieving a degree of carelessness he certainly didn't feel. 'You might know more about them than me.'

'Y—e—s.'

Lily swallowed, hardly daring to believe what she was hearing. That Dee-Dee had sensed she was in danger. She would have to thank her, she thought a little uneasily. But she probably wouldn't mention her amateurish attempt to contact Dee-Dee, even so.

'She must have second sight.'

'*De veras*. Indeed,' agreed Rafe unsteadily. 'Having just discovered how much you mean to me, I could not bear it if I had lost you. If you had died, I would have wanted to die too.'

Lily gazed at him. 'Do you mean that?'

'I mean it,' he assured her huskily, and then gave in to the desire to bury his face in the soft curve of her neck. 'I love you, Lily. I know it is too soon and I should wait until you are stronger, but I want you to know how I feel about you. I want us to be together, *querida*. I want to marry you. I never want to take the chance of losing you again.'

For a significant while there was silence in the room.

Although Rafe was torn—after all, he hadn't had a shower or a shave in over twenty-four hours—when Lily wound her arms about his neck, he couldn't resist.

His protests, that the nurse might appear at any time or that her father might choose to call at Orchid Point before conducting his morning service, were easily stifled by the eager pressure of her mouth. They were hungry for one another, and all he could hear was the blood hammering through his veins and the matching pulsing of her heart.

Eventually, when it became obvious that Lily was no longer in control of her emotions, Rafe forced himself to draw back.

'I think it is time I let the nurse know you are

awake,' he said, swallowing convulsively. 'Will you be all right?'

'I'll have to be, won't I?' murmured Lily ruefully, but her eyes were dancing, and Rafe bent to take her lips one more time before getting to his feet.

'I will be back as soon as I have made myself decent,' he promised, and Lily giggled at the image that evoked.

'You are decent,' she insisted, sobering. 'You are a decent man and that is why I love you.'

'Lily!'

His voice was hoarse and, realising she was being cruel by tormenting him, she ran gentle fingers across his thigh. 'Would you kiss me? Please,' she whispered, 'before you go. Just to convince me that this isn't a dream.'

Rafe's eyes darkened but, before he could make good on her request, the door opened to admit the nurse. She looked momentarily taken aback when she saw them together. But, like the good nurse she was, she managed a polite smile.

'I see Ms Fielding's awake,' she said crisply. She paused. 'But, if you don't mind, Mr Oliveira, I'd prefer to examine my patient alone.'

EPILOGUE

RAFE AND LILY flew to Europe for a belated honeymoon three months later.

They'd been married for six weeks but, what with the fallout from the explosion and the official investigation, it hadn't been possible for them to get away any sooner.

Sarah's parents had arrived to take their daughter's remains home for burial. Her father, who owned a small restaurant in New York, had been subdued but philosophical.

Despite his obvious grief, he'd been prepared to accept that his daughter had been a sick girl. He admitted he'd suspected something was wrong even before she'd married Rafe.

Her mother was more concerned with what was going to happen to the apartment where Sarah had been living. It was still Rafe's apartment although, as he explained to Lily, he'd moved out long ago.

'It is yours,' he'd said with his usual generosity,

causing Mrs Hilton to burst into tears at his words. 'Do what you like with it. I never want to see it again.'

When the Hiltons had departed there'd been Ray to deal with. The explosion had caused a fire which had damaged two other boats, and naturally he'd had no insurance to cover his losses.

He was immensely relieved when Rafe formalised his partnership in the agency and made good on all the debts Ray had accrued since the accident. But Rafe told Lily he intended to ensure the business was run on a much more professional basis from now on.

'So I assume we are going to live on the island?' Lily had said before the wedding, and Rafe had regarded her with curious eyes.

'You would rather live somewhere else?' he'd queried in some surprise. 'Well, we can do that. We can live wherever you like—so long as we are together.'

Lily had wrapped her arms around him then. 'Of course I don't want to live anywhere else,' she'd assured him. 'And you know how relieved my father will be at this news. I was afraid you might be getting bored with island life.'

Rafe shook his head. 'Is this because I have let Grant Mathews have his plantation back at a reduced sum?' he queried. He pulled a wry face. 'I just thought the poor man deserved a break. With a daughter like Laura to contend with...' He didn't continue. 'And I have so much, why should I begrudge him a bit of happiness?'

'You're too generous,' said Lily fervently. After

the way Laura had behaved, she still found it hard
to feel charitable towards either of the Mathewses.
'But I don't mind. It's just another of the things I
love about you.'

'And the other things would be…?' Rafe enquired,
bending to nip her ear with his teeth.

'You'll find out,' retorted Lily a little unsteadily.
'Now, behave yourself. Daddy is coming to supper.'

The trip to Europe was as marvellous as Lily had
anticipated. They spent a week in London, visiting
her mother's sister and seeing the sights, and then
moved on to Paris and Rome.

It was nearing Christmas and it was cold, but it
meant they could explore the cities at their own pace.
There were no queues, no crowds, no hustle. Just the
two of them in a magical world of their own.

On their last night in Rome they had dinner at
their favourite trattoria and then walked back to their
hotel with the floodlit walls of the ancient Roman
Forum providing an enchanted backdrop.

They were returning home the following day,
but Lily wasn't downhearted. Although they'd had
a wonderful four weeks, it would be good to see familiar faces and familiar places again.

In their suite, Lily went straight into the bedroom
and shed her coat and scarf before dropping lazily
onto the bed. She kicked off her shoes and spread
her arms and legs in total abandon. She felt mildly
tipsy from the rich Italian wine she'd been drinking

and when Rafe appeared in the doorway she beck-oned him to come and join her.

Rafe dropped his long cashmere coat and leather jacket onto a wooden ottoman at the foot of the bed, and then came to look down at her. He was wearing a cream silk shirt and now he loosened the collar and pulled his tie away from his neck.

'You look—wanton,' he said, kneeling on the bed beside her and placing his hands on the satin coverlet at either side of her head. 'Totally wanton.'

'So long as you want me,' whispered Lily huskily, allowing her fingers to stroke his jawline that was already roughening with his beard. And Rafe caught his breath at the knowing provocation.

'Oh, I want you, *querida*,' he muttered, lowering his head to lick the scented hollow of her cleavage. 'More each time I make love with you.'

Lily shivered in delicious anticipation. The erotic abrasion of his tongue only accentuated the need that had been building inside her all evening, and she curled a languid arm around his neck.

'Come here,' she commanded, and Rafe trailed a sensual path of kisses to the curve of her jawline and the parted sweetness of her lips.

But he didn't lower his body onto hers. Although she was aching for him to do so, he drew back in-stead and tipped the straps of her green and gold chiffon dress off her shoulders.

Immediately, the rounded fullness of her breasts

were exposed to his heavy-lidded gaze and he made a hoarse sound of satisfaction.

'*Hermosa,*' he said thickly. 'You are so beautiful.' He allowed his fingers to trace the dusky circle around her nipple and smiled when she arched up against him. 'Do not be impatient, *niña*. I want to taste you first.'

Her dress and the lacy panties beneath it were soon discarded. By the time Rafe had torn off his shirt and suede trousers, Lily was shifting restlessly against the scarlet coverlet.

But Rafe was in no hurry to satisfy her urgency. Taking his time bestowing kisses from the soles of her feet, up the inner curve of her thigh to the moist place that pulsed between her legs, he prolonged his own provocation.

Spreading her legs wider, Rafe explored her with his tongue, and she felt the rushing heat of her orgasm invade his open mouth. Then, when she was weak and panting from her body's exertions, he moved lazily onward.

He traced the hollow of her navel and the gentle indentation of her waist before finding the undersides of her breasts. Lily had dabbed perfume there and it mingled with the womanly scent of her arousal, causing Rafe to growl with sensual pleasure.

Her nipples were next and he suckled at each of them in turn, using his teeth and his tongue to bring her to the edge of another climax.

This time, she wouldn't let him make the pace,

however. With unconscious sensuality, she wound her legs about him, bringing the throbbing heat of his erection close against the moist curls of her mound.

'Please,' she begged, reaching down to cup him with her hands, and Rafe sucked in a tortured breath.

'Okay, okay,' he said hoarsely, pulling back to ease his aching crotch. 'You win, *querida*.' And, with the familiarity of their shared experience, Lily guided him into her hot sheath.

Their lovemaking was as amazing as always. Rafe thought he would never tire of burying himself in her sweetness, of not knowing where his body ended and hers began.

He was completely and utterly enchanted by his new wife and he loved her so much he didn't believe it was possible to love her more.

They arrived back at Orchid Point in the early hours of the morning.

Despite his generosity towards the Mathewses, Rafe had retained possession of the house they had both come to regard as their home. Orchid Point held a special place in their hearts and Lily wouldn't have it any other way.

In spite of the lateness of the hour, both Carla and Steve were there to greet them and Lily thought how wonderful it was to climb into their own bed again.

The following day they went to visit her father. As Lily had anticipated, the Reverend Fielding had been delighted to learn they were to stay on the island, and he welcomed them back with more enthusiasm than was usual for him.

While Rafe was sharing a drink with her father, Lily went to find Dee-Dee. She and the West Indian woman had talked little about the accident at the marina. Before they went away, the subject had been too raw, too painful. But now, like Carla and Steve before her, she was eager to see the young woman who'd been like a daughter to her for so many years.

'You look so well, girl,' she exclaimed after hugging her warmly. 'But that's how it happens sometimes.'

'How what happens?' Lily was curious. 'Being married agrees with me. If that's what you mean.'

'And the rest,' retorted Dee-Dee, her expression humorous. 'When were you planning on telling your Daddy?'

'Telling Daddy what? Rafe's with him now, giving him the low-down of where we've been and what we've seen while we were away.' She grinned. 'It's amazing how quickly Daddy has taken to Rafe as his son-in-law.'

Dee-Dee stared at her. 'Are you telling me you don't know what I'm talking about, girl? After the way you got a message to me about that mad woman at the marina, I felt sure you'd know exactly what I mean.'

'No.' Lily was diverted. Then, tentatively, 'You mean I did communicate my fears to you?'

'How else would I have known what was going

on?' Dee-Dee was dismissive. 'I got one of my fa-
mous feelings, didn't I? Anyway, your Mr Oliveira
didn't need a second warning.'

'Thank goodness!' Lily's words were heartfelt.
'So are you saying that you think I should tell Daddy
what happened?'

'No!' Dee-Dee gasped. 'Did I say you should tell
the Reverend? I did not.'

'Then what?'

Dee-Dee shook her head now. Then she came towards the girl and ran her hand over Lily's stomach.
'I guess it hasn't affected you yet.'

Lily stared at her for a long moment before comprehension dawned. When Dee-Dee removed her
hand, Lily put her own hand in its place.

Where once her stomach had been only slightly
rounded, now a distinct firmness swelled beneath
her cotton shorts.

'I'm pregnant?' she ventured with a certain air of
wonder. And then caught her breath on the words as
Rafe came into the kitchen to join them.

'Did I miss something?' he asked, looking from
Dee-Dee's smug countenance to his wife's suddenly
flushed face, and Lily gave an incredulous shake of
her head.

'Not a thing,' she said firmly, slipping her arm
through his. 'Did you have a nice chat with Daddy?'

'Sí.' But Rafe still looked suspicious. 'He sent me
to ask if we can have some coffee.' His eyes dark-

ened as he took in her excited face. 'What's going
on? Is something wrong?'

'Unless the fact that you're going to be a daddy
yourself shortly doesn't appeal,' Lily told him lightly,
and waited for his response.

But the incredulous delight on Rafe's face said
it all.

* * * * *

If you enjoyed
A DANGEROUS TASTE OF PASSION,
look out for these other great reads
by Anne Mather!

MORELLI'S MISTRESS
A FORBIDDEN TEMPTATION
INNOCENT VIRGIN, WILD SURRENDER
HIS FORBIDDEN PASSION
THE BRAZILIAN MILLIONAIRE'S LOVE-CHILD
Available now!

COMING NEXT MONTH FROM

HARLEQUIN

Presents.

Available January 17, 2017

#3497 THE LAST DI SIONE CLAIMS HIS PRIZE
The Billionaire's Legacy
by Maisey Yates
Even unsentimental Alessandro Di Sione can't deny his
grandfather's dream of retrieving a scandalous painting. Yet
its return depends on outspoken Princess Gabriella. While
traveling together to locate the painting, Gabby is drawn to this
guilt-ridden man. Could their passion be his salvation?

#3498 THE DESERT KING'S BLACKMAILED BRIDE
Brides for the Taking
by Lynne Graham
Naive Polly Dixon lands in the desert kingdom of Dharia
clutching an ornate ring—and finds herself arrested! Carrying
the ring has led King Rashad's people to believe that Polly
is his long-awaited bride—so Rashad begins a fiery sensual
onslaught...

#3499 THE CONSEQUENCE OF HIS VENGEANCE
One Night With Consequences
by Jennie Lucas
Letty Spencer's father once forced her to push away
Darius Kyrillos. A decade later, he's come back to claim her.
But revenge soon melts into insatiable need. And when Darius
discovers his impending fatherhood, he won't allow Letty to
dismiss the heat between them...

#3500 BOUGHT TO WEAR THE BILLIONAIRE'S RING
by Cathy Williams
Samantha Wilson never forgot Leo Morgan-White's rejection.
But now he'll absolve her mother's debts if Samantha will pose
as his fiancée. It won't be long before their agreement comes to
an end, but Sam's resistance is buckling under the heat of Leo's
expert touch...

HPCNM0117RA

#3501 BRIDE BY ROYAL DECREE
Wedlocked!
by Caitlin Crews

King Reza's betrothed, Princess Magdalena, disappeared years ago. But a mysterious photograph brings them together again. Fiercely independent Maggy won't accept her birthright on any terms but her own—so Reza will have to use sensual persuasions that Maggy will be helpless to resist!

#3502 THE SHEIKH'S SECRET SON
Secret Heirs of Billionaires
by Maggie Cox

Sheikh Zafir el-Kalil will do anything to secure his child—even marry the woman who kept their son a secret! But Darcy Carrick is older and wiser now, and it will take more than soft words and sweet seduction to win back her love...

#3503 ACQUIRED BY HER GREEK BOSS
by Chantelle Shaw

Greek tycoon Alekos Gionakis thinks he knows his secretary, until he's forced to reappraise his most precious asset! Alekos offers beautiful Sara Lovejoy a meeting with her unknown family, provided she agrees to become his mistress. But Sara's innocence is priceless...

#3504 VOWS THEY CAN'T ESCAPE
by Heidi Rice

Xanthe Carmichael has discovered two things: that she's *still* married, and her husband could take half her business! Xanthe is hit by lust when she confronts him with divorce papers...but will Dane begin stirring the smoldering embers of their passion?

YOU CAN FIND MORE INFORMATION ON UPCOMING HARLEQUIN® TITLES, FREE EXCERPTS AND MORE AT WWW.HARLEQUIN.COM.

HPCNM0117RB

HARLEQUIN
Presents.

**Don't miss Heidi Rice's thrilling
Harlequin Presents debut—a story of
a couple tempestuously reunited!**

Xanthe Carmichael has just discovered two things:
1. Her ex-husband could take half her business
2. She's actually still married to him!

When she jets off to New York, divorce papers in hand, Xanthe
is prepared for the billionaire bad boy's slick offices…but not for
the spear of lust that hits her the moment she sees Dane Redmond
again! Has her body no shame, no recollection of the pain he
caused? But Dane is stalling… Is he really checking the fine print
or planning to stir the smoldering embers of their passion and
tempt her back into the marriage bed?

Don't miss

VOWS THEY CAN'T ESCAPE

Available February 2017

Stay Connected:

www.Harlequin.com

/HarlequinBooks

@HarlequinBooks

/HarlequinBooks

HP06044

SPECIAL EXCERPT FROM

Even unsentimental Alessandro Di Sione can't deny his
grandfather's dream of retrieving a scandalous painting.
Yet its return depends on outspoken Princess Gabriella.
While traveling together to locate the painting, Gabby
is drawn to this guilt-ridden man. Could their passion
be his salvation?

Read on for a sneak preview of
THE LAST DI SIONE CLAIMS HIS PRIZE
the final part in the unmissable new eight-book
Harlequin Presents® series
THE BILLIONAIRE'S LEGACY

Alessandro was so different than she was. Gabby had
never truly fully appreciated just how different men and
women were. In a million ways, big and small.

Yes, there was the obvious, but it was more than that.
And it was those differences that suddenly caused her to
glory in who she was, what she was. To feel, if only for
a moment, that she completely understood herself both
body and soul, and that they were united in one desire.

"Kiss me, Princess," he said, his voice low, strained.

He was affected.

So she had won.

She had been the one to make him burn.

But she'd made a mistake if she'd thought this game
had one winner and one loser. She was right down there
with him. And she didn't care about winning anymore.

She couldn't deny him, not now. Not when he was

looking at her like she was a woman and not a girl, or an owl. Not when he was looking at her like she was the sun, moon and all the stars combined. Bright, brilliant and something that held the power to hold him transfixed.

Something more than what she was. Because Gabriella D'Oro had never transfixed anyone. Not her parents. Not a man.

But he was looking at her like she mattered. She didn't feel like shrinking into a wall or melting into the scenery. She wanted him to keep looking.

She didn't want to hide from this. She wanted all of it.

Slowly, so slowly, so that she could savor the feel of him, relish the sensations of his body beneath her touch, she slid her hand up his throat, feeling the heat of his skin, the faint scratch of whiskers.

Then she moved to cup his jaw, his cheek.

"I've never touched a man like this before," she confessed.

And she wasn't even embarrassed by the confession, because he was still looking at her like he wanted her.

He moved closer, covering her hand with his. She could feel his heart pounding heavily, could sense the tension running through his frame. "I've touched a great many women," he said, his tone grave. "But at the moment it doesn't seem to matter."

That was when she kissed him.

Don't miss
THE LAST DI SIONE CLAIMS HIS PRIZE,
available February 2017 wherever
Harlequin Presents® books and ebooks are sold.

www.Harlequin.com

Copyright © 2017 by Harlequin Books S.A.

HPEXP0117